T0170987

SHE'LL GET WHAT'S COMING TO HER!

Her real name was Vicky Hustin, but to the people of Big Hominy she would always be "that uppity mountain gal, that piece of hill trash who thinks she's so high and mighty." And when her ex-husband was found brutally murdered, they had still another name for her: Man-killer!

They also had a name for someone like Wade Calhoun, who dared to believe in Vicky's innocence. Crazy, that's what he was. Shell-shocked from the war, probably. Just ignore him till the trial's over and that no-good gal's had her comeuppance on the gallows!

But Wade Calhoun wasn't giving up that easily. He'd turn up the one bit of evidence the town couldn't ignore. Because even if it meant pitting his life against that of a killer, he was determined once and for all to balance the scales of Big Hominy's justice!

Man-Killer

Talmadge Powell

Adams Media

New York London Toronto Sydney New Delhi

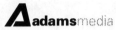

Adams Media
An Imprint of Simon & Schuster, Inc.
57 Littlefield Street
Avon, Massachusetts 02322

ADAMS MEDIA and colophon are trademarks of Simon & Schuster, Inc.

For information about special discounts for bulk purchases, please contact Simon
& Schuster Special Sales at 1-866-506-1949 or business@simonandschuster.com.

Manufactured in the United States of America

Library of Congress Cataloging-in-Publication Data has been applied for.

ISBN 978-1-4405-5520-6
ISBN 978-1-4405-3691-5 (ebook)

This work has been previously published in print format by Ace Books, Inc.

1.

AT LAST a spider came to the silent brush screening me and began trying to spin a web. She hung from a gossamer thread, trying to swing to a twig and anchor the skein. Each time she was uncessful. Then I added a gust of my breath to the thin mountain breeze. It gave the spider the necessary impetus, but it was the wrong thing to do. It was an artificial factor forced into the natural order of things. My movement was something out of the Unknown; and now the spider hung clumped into a tight ball at the end of her thread. She would never spin a web in this place.

I turned my attention from the spider. The Winchester was heavy across my knees. The late shadows were picking up a chill. Above me the damp, cool, wooded mountain strained toward the sky. A hundred yards below ran the narrow ledge of road. Beyond that, the mountain dropped dizzily toward a valley half hidden by the blue mists of twilight.

Far down in the valley a feeble finger of smoke wavered toward the sky as a hill woman started corn pone and collards for supper. A faint gray cloud formed across the yawning distance, moving across the face of the mountain beyond the valley. The dust smudge, I knew, was stirred up by a moving car. This time it had to be Clarence Oldham's car and not a muddy pickup truck or rattling Ford. I didn't think I could stand the waiting much longer.

5

MAN-KILLER

As the keening sound of the car's motor insinuated itself into the mountain stillness, I brought the Winchester from its resting place on my knees. Through rifts in the brush I commanded a good view of the road, but looking into the brush from the road a person would have a hard time seeing enough of me for recognition.

I knew Vicky would be sitting beside Oldham as he drove, and I wondered if at this very moment she was laughing at something he was saying.

The car came around a curve with a speed and deftness sufficient to make me admire Oldham's driving in this terrain, lowlander that he was.

The car was a black sedan, and I squeezed the trigger of the Winchester and laid a bright furrow across the left front fender of the car. Oldham jammed on the brakes when the gun crashed, and the car slithered to a stop in a cloud of dust.

I had clean creek gravel in my pocket. I popped it in my mouth and yelled, "Get out, both of you!"

Oldham hesitated, saying something to Vicky. Then he got out of the car alone. "What is this, a mountain stick-up?"

There was just enough of a sneer in his voice to have got him killed if it had been a hooger pulling a heist. I had to admire his nerve, although I wasn't too surprised by it. From the time he'd first showed up in Big Hominy, I'd pegged him for a cool, arrogant fish.

I didn't want to talk much, and I wished Oldham weren't so cool. The mouthful of pebbles was only a partial disguise for my voice.

"I told both of you to get out," I yelled.

Vicky slipped out of the car.

"That's better," I shouted. "Now you come up here, Mrs. Hustin."

"Listen," Oldham said, "if it's money you want—"

"It isn't. So save your breath. I don't want to hurt anybody. I want to give Mrs. Hustin a message from her husband."

She and Oldham traded a glance; then she moved away from the car, slipping once as she started up the steep embankment from the road. The sun was at her back and she seemed to be etched in red fire, with the mountain breeze skipping through the burnished copper of her hair. She was taller and more slender than most hill women, and for my money more beautiful than any woman anywhere.

She walked to the thicket and said, "Wade!"

"Not so loud."

A flash of anger touched her eyes. "Are you drunk, Wade?"

"No."

"Then what kind of prank—"

"It's no prank. Something has happened to Rock Hustin and I don't want you going back to town right now."

She looked at me a moment, and when her voice came it was very quiet. "Are you trying to tell me that Rock is sick or hurt, Wade? I'm through with him. I've been through with him for a long time. What could I do to help him?"

"Not him. Yourself."

"You needn't be afraid for me. There's nothing he can do to hurt me."

"I wish that were true. How I wish it!"

From the road, Oldham yelled, "What is it, Vicky? I'm coming up there."

7

"You take one step," I called, "and I'll break your knees with rifle slugs."

Vicky gave me a look that meant she was sore at me. "Wade, I'm going back to the car. Mr. Oldham isn't used to this kind of thing."

"You won't ever believe me or trust me, will you, Vicky? Okay, here it is. Rock was murdered last night at Deaf Joyner's fish camp. His body was found late this morning."

It took a second for her mind to absorb it. Then she went pale and a shiver coursed over her body. She closed her eyes. "Rock is dead," she said in a shaky voice, "and I don't feel any tears, Wade. Isn't that rotten of me?"

"But you're crying."

"Only for myself. Only because I've grown so callous I don't feel sad over a man's death. Wade, I don't want to be a mean or cruel person. I want to feel tender and gentle and clean inside, where it matters."

I knew what she was trying to express. She was begging life not to beat her down any more, not to warp or twist her. Looking at the blind plea in her face, I felt as if I wanted to strike and break something. A man, a law, anything.

She rubbed her palm across her cheek. "Thanks for telling me, Wade. I'll go now."

I looked away from her, staring at Oldham down there in the road. "You can't go," I said. "They're looking for you. They think you killed Rock."

I heard the intake of her breath. I knew she was looking at me with the knowledge in her heart that I wasn't kidding about this, that I had made sure before I came here.

"Wade, what'll I do?"

"Go back down there and send Oldham on alone. Tell

8

him I'm a cousin. Tell him you've got to meet Rock. Tell him the truth, anything, but get rid of him so I can take you to a place where you'll be safe until I have a chance to do something."

"No, I think I'd better go back, Wade, and face it. I can straighten it out. I didn't kill Rock."

"They think you did. Sheriff Hyder has a case against you. You've been tried and convicted over every backyard fence in Big Hominy. What do you want to do, provide them with a Roman holiday? Now get down there and get rid of Oldham."

I heard her take one slow step; another. I glanced at her, and she was moving toward the road like a mechanical doll with no feeling in it.

She reached the cutbank. Oldham helped her down, taking both her hands in his, and throwing a mean-mad glance in my direction. He pulled her close to him and they talked for a minute.

There was little doubt in my mind as to Clarence Oldham's serious and honorable intentions toward Vicky. He had money and class. He was in the mountains for a vacation. He was not the kind of man you'd associate with the usual hill girl. But Vicky was different. He sensed it; he saw the qualities in her that I did, and he treated her like a gentleman. Big Hominy didn't like that, having its own opinion of how she should be treated.

Oldham's argument with her failed. He got in his car and drove off.

I crawled out of the brambles as she came up the slope; she moved as if she were tired, and her face was lined with frustration.

9

I spat out the pebbles. "What did Oldham have to say?"

"He tried to talk me out of it."

"What did you tell him?"

"That Rock was dead. The truth, Wade, except I didn't identify you."

She looked at her high-heeled shoes, and then up the mountainside. She sat down, took the shoes off, and peeled her nylons from her legs. "Maybe I should have listened to him, Wade. He said it was crazy for me even to think I'd get blamed for Rock's death. Clarence said he would hire a good lawyer. I'd get nowhere running away, he said. I hurt him, Wade, and he's been nice to me."

"He doesn't know Big Hominy, though."

"No, he doesn't. Well, what do we do now?"

"I'll take you across the mountain to the old Stillman place. The cabin is still sound enough for you to be comfortable there this time of year."

We climbed up through the timber, following a dim trail that most eyes would have missed. But we were both hill bred, and the trail was as plain to us as a city sidewalk. The cool breath of the mountains was in our faces and the solitude wrapped us. It could have been nice, having her walk beside me this way.

"You haven't told me about Rock," she said, and her voice was so tight it jarred me with an awareness of the feelings she must be fighting to control.

"Deaf Joyner found Rock this morning when he took a bottle of whisky to the cabin where Rock's been staying. Deaf reported the killing and Sheriff Hyder took Doc Braddock up with him. The doctor said Rock was killed about eleven o'clock last night by a blow on the head. Deaf said he'd seen

10

a woman come out of the cabin about that time. She'd run through the glade below the cabin and moonlight had struck her full in the face. Deaf said the woman was you."

She faltered a step, then kept on walking.

"Deaf said he just figured you'd paid a visit to your ex-husband, and he thought nothing about it until this morning. Kirk Hyder spotted the fireplace poker lying across the cabin from the fireplace, and wondered if it could have been the murder weapon. He wrapped it up, along with a compact and a couple of other things that he took from your room, and sent a deputy highsailing it to Asheville.

"The deputy was all steamed up when he got back with news that the Identification Bureau in Asheville had matched up fingerprints from your things with a set from the poker."

I glanced at her, but her bloodless face remained a silent mask.

"The minute I heard," I said, "I went to the employees' quarters at the hotel. You'd left early in the morning with Oldham and no one knew where you had gone. I bribed a maid to let me in the room. I saw nothing more than Kirk had, but I put two things together. There was a purchase slip from Brudick's, dated yesterday, for a new bathing suit. I couldn't find the suit.

"I decided you and Oldham had gone to Cheoah Park for the day, planning to swim, maybe go boating. It was the only thing I could think of.

"I was afraid to go to Cheoah because you might take the Burnston road back and I'd miss you. So I holed up east of the point where the Burnston and Big Hominy roads join. If you'd been to Cheeoah, you had to come back along that stretch."

11

She stopped walking. There was an old log lying beside
the path, and she sat down on it, resting her elbows on her
knees, letting her hands fall limp.

"It's no good, Wade."

"Don't talk crazy!"

"You tried—thanks. It would have been better if you'd
let me walk into it."

I sat down beside her, took her chin in my hand, and
made her look at me.

"I haven't started to try yet, Vicky. There's just one thing
I must know. Did you kill Rock? You said back there that
you didn't. But I want to hear it again, with you looking in
my eyes. Did you kill him, Vicky?"

"Before God, Wade, I swear to you that I didn't."

I nodded. I didn't care what the evidence said. I knew her
too well. I knew she couldn't tell that kind of lie while
she was looking at me like that.

"Was Deaf lying about you being in the cabin?"

"No," she said. "I was there."

"You shouldn't have gone."

She read the blame in my eyes and dropped her head as
if ready to accept punishment. "I know it, Wade. Just another
two months now and I could have got my divorce under
the two-year separation law. I hadn't seen Rock since he'd
been back. I didn't know for sure that he was back, just
heard gossip that he was hanging around the fish camps and
bootlegging joints. Then he sent word to me that he was in
trouble and had to see me. I was afraid not to go to Joyner's.
You know how Rock was."

A brute. That was Rock.

"He was dead when I got there," Vicky said. "Alone with

12

him, I got scared. I thought I heard somebody moving around outside the cabin—that's when I picked up the poker. I didn't know if it was really somebody or just nerves. As soon as the night was still again, I threw down the poker and ran like crazy. I didn't think of fingerprints or anything except getting away. When I got to my room I calmed down. I knew what people were bound to say when Rock was found. But saying isn't proving, and this morning I decided the best thing was to go on about my business as if I'd never been out there. In the light of day, it was easy to convince myself that all I'd heard last night was leaves rustling outside the cabin."

She stared down into the darkening valley. "I'm tired of fighting, Wade. I've kidded myself too long. I'm just Hap McCall's daughter, hill trash. Even animals in cages have more sense—they don't try to beat their brains out against the bars. It would be a relief to just give up."

"I won't let you," I said. "And I won't let them hurt you any more either."

She studied my face. "No," she said. "You're sincere right now, Wade, and I believe you. But later . . ."

"Come on," I said. "It's time we were getting to the old Stillman place."

With a shrug, she started up the trail ahead of me, carrying her shoes and stockings. Without looking over her shoulder, she asked, "What are your plans?"

"To leave you hidden and safe, while I turn up something in Big Hominy. If I can't . . ."

"Yes, Wade?"

"I'll get together all the money I can and take you out of the country."

She kept walking without saying anything and finally I said angrily, "Maybe you wish it was Oldham taking you."

"He treated me nice, Wade. He has a business of his own in Charlotte. He can afford to spend three or four hundred dollars vacationing at the hotel. He might even have asked me to marry him, but he won't now. So I wasn't wishing anything about Clarence."

The flat sound of her voice reminded me of the dry rustling of leaves blowing across a mountainside on a winter day.

I began cussing softly and steadily under my breath.

Nothing mattered to her any more.

2

VICKY WAS born with two strikes against her.

She was one of Hap McCall's brood. She was born into hill trash. I used to see her in Big Hominy when Hap brought his tired, work-worn wife and passel of kids to town in a wagon held together with bailing wire.

They were a sorry, sad, shiftless lot, but Vicky was different. She was ashamed, and fiercely proud. Her eyes reflected intelligence, and she was beautiful.

I was born within forty miles of the mountain where Hap moonshined and worked his rocky farm, but I was born into a different world. I was a Calhoun.

True, the glory of the Calhoun name was as dim as the shuttered, memory-haunted rooms in the main part of the once-fine house my mother had closed after the bank manipulation and my father's suicide. But my mother was one of those silken-strong women peculiar to an older era in the South. As mortgages ate away the Calhoun land, she never lost hope, nor forgot that she was a Gilliam married into the Calhoun line.

Big Hominy never forgot either. They judged my father gently, especially after it was learned that he had been trying to bring the railroad in. Big Hominy might have been more kindly to me too, but I had a wrong foot forward. I flunked out of Riverdale, the military academy where Calhouns had gone back to the time of Colonel Judd, the Calhoun at Lee's left hand at Appomattox Courthouse. And somewhere along the line I developed a veneer of aggressiveness to cover the

15

fact that I was never far from the sight of Calhoun poverty and the way my father had died.

I guess I had Vicky in my blood for a long time. I used to think about her during my army hitch, which ended during rear echelon duty in Korea before I ever got to the front.

When I came back stateside I got tanked up and went up to Spivey Mountain to see her. I loused that up the way I had a lot of things. I was a Calhoun on a binge, out to find some easy pickings among the hill trash. That's the way I guess she must have felt. It wasn't the way I felt, but she never did trust me after that.

Rock Hustin was seven years her senior when Hap McCall forced her to marry him. I didn't learn and didn't care to know what method Hap used. But I did know that Rock gave Hap three hundred dollars when the wedding was over. Hap used the money to buy a flivver and get drunk. He ended in a junk heap of metal at the bottom of a mountainside, losing his left eye and most of that side of his face. He almost bled to death by the time he crawled home.

Rock was a pathological criminal. He took Vicky across the mountain into Tennessee, got in a shooting scrape and had to leave the country.

Vicky got a job in Knoxville, returning only when her mother broke her hip. The return was a compromise. Nothing could chain her to Spivey Mountain again. She helped her mother through the illness and got a job in the Stonewall Jackson Hotel as a dining-room hostess. Once or twice a month she would go to the McCall place to give her mother what help she could. Always she took along candy, dress material, and gifts for the kids.

MAN-KILLER

Big Hominy talked about her for a while and at first there were men who considered her fair prey. She moved through it all with a quiet, natural dignity.

I saw her every time she would let me. Big Hominy saw us and talked. My mother was bewildered. I begged Vicky to marry me as soon as her divorce was final.

"I'm too old for you, Wade."

"I beat you into this world by three years."

"I wasn't talking about that kind of oldness."

She would sit quiet and remote sometimes as we drove up to the Stonewall Jackson, the rambling old resort hotel overlooking Big Hominy.

Sometimes she warmed to my kisses, and sometimes she pushed me away.

"You drink too much, Wade."

"I'll quit."

"You quit last week and the week before that."

Some nights I didn't sleep well but lay seething with hatred of Rock Hustin because of the scars he'd left behind. I wondered if she'd ever trust a man again.

Word trickled through the hills that Rock was back. Vicky didn't show fear, but I knew it was there.

Clarence Oldham came to the hotel with his conservative black car, his cool, assured manner, his tailored hunting togs.

"I'm losing you," I told her. We'd driven out to Bit Barney's Bar-B-Cue for supper, and I'd parked later on the mountain above the hotel.

"You don't have any claims on me, Wade."

"The claim of my feelings. That's all. That's enough."

"I'm fond of Clarence, Wade."

"And he can give you the kind of life you're after?"

Moonlight had given her face a haunted look. "I think we'd better go now."

The next day Rock was dead. Talk of it was all over town. Kirk Hyder didn't have her in jail. Kirk Hyder hadn't been able to find her. She'd gone off with Clarence Oldham early in the morning. Big Hominy gasped and talked, and the air was electric. The waiting and foretelling were over. Blood had told. She had lived down to her name.

Faces swam by me. Snatches of talk gave me the facts of Rock's death, the case against her. The flesh grew tight across my shoulders.

I'll find them. I'll take her from Oldham. I'll run further than Oldham would ever dream of running. Fight in ways Oldham would never imagine.

I am her only real hope.

She's mine now.

3

THE OLD Stillman cabin was nestled in a glade just over the crest of the mountain. I was aware of Vicky's nearness and warmth as we entered the ramshackle house. I lighted a Coleman lantern I'd brought up with me. Its soft hissing quietly accented the sighing of the night breeze through the trees outside.

In the lantern glow, the interior of the cabin was revealed, the rough, worm-eaten logs, the hard dirt floor, the sagging timbers of the roof. A rusty iron bed and stove and a hand-hewn table still stood in the cabin, which had been un-occupied since the death of old man Stillman.

Vicky looked at the canned goods I'd dumped on the table. My car was hidden in a grove of trees below the cabin. I'd stopped here first with supplies before crossing the peak to intercept her and Oldham.

"Are you hungry, Wade?"

"I could eat. I'll start a fire."

While I set the stove to smoking, she took stuff out of the corrugated cardboard box on the table—canned meat, beans, coffee, bread, two pots and a skillet, a package of paper plates and another of wooden picnic spoons.

I lit a cigarette and watched Vicky open beans and Spam. She put the beans on to heat. Water was the only item I'd forgotten, and I picked up the second pot, went outside to the spring above the house.

I carried the water back and she put coffee on to boil. She moved about the stove as her mother would move, as count-

less generations of hill women had moved, not because hope
was the mainspring, but only because the heart kept beating,
the lungs kept breathing, and the hands, feet, and body went
through the motions of living without knowing why.

After we ate, I said, "You can't stay here long. Oldham
will tell Kirk Hyder what happened and the sheriff will scour
the hills around the spot where you were taken from Oldham's car. You've got until daylight to rest. I want you out
of here before dawn. Take the food with you. Don't leave
any sign that you've been here. You'll have to hide all day
and maybe do a lot of running to keep out of Hyder's way.
You will stay out of his reach, won't you?"

She studied my face.

"Hyder," I said, "won't have a chance of catching you in
these hills if you make up your mind not to let him."

"All right, Wade, I'll stay out of his reach."

"Then return here tomorrow night. I'll meet you. We'll
kiss these mountains good-bye forever, Vicky." I took her
hands in mine. "You see what that means? A new start. A
brand new life."

"You won't get drunk or make any mistakes?"

"How many times do I have to tell you?" I gave her the
Winchester, moved toward the door.

She followed me. I kissed her, and there was a faint
warmth in her lips.

She stood in the cabin doorway, watching me go. Crickets
skirled their mating cries and a night creature in the distance
screamed at the new-risen moon. The mountain night would
have frightened a lot of women, but it had no power over her.
Her fears were composed of different things. The rifle would
protect her from things which held no fear, animate things.

MAN - KILLER

I drove fast all the way back to Big Hominy. I flashed through a residential section where time had tiptoed past the hulking, gingerbread houses. The business district was lonely, deserted, with street lamps throwing pale yellow pools over the secretive streets.

I swung around the square where the monument to the county's Confederate War dead stood. The courthouse was on the west side of the square, a decaying brick building with a dome copied from the capitol in Washington. The courthouse clock was tolling eleven-thirty, and there were lights on the ground floor where Kirk Hyder had his office.

I drove on out to the house, approaching it along the weed-grown driveway sheltered by tall poplar trees. The lights in Kirk's office had made me think he was there. He wasn't. He was here. Because of the trees I didn't see the car parked before the house until I was right on it.

The car blocked the driveway, and Kirk Hyder was standing beside it.

I stopped the jalopy and got out. The light on our broad veranda flashed on, and my mother, a shawl around her shoulders, stepped to the driveway and came toward me.

Kirk Hyder said howdy. He had been sheriff ever since I could remember. He was as lean as a slab-sided hound and had a face about as attractive. His iron gray hair stood like a brush on his head, and his eyes, blue and calm, were forever unreadable.

"Where's the girl, Wade?" Kirk asked.

"Which girl?"

"You know who I'm talking about. Vicky Hustin. Where'd you take her?"

"I haven't seen her."

21

MAN - KILLER

My mother was standing close to us. "You see, Sheriff? You'll have to look elsewhere. I told you Wade wouldn't do a thing like that."

"Kirk," I said, "I'm too tired for games. I'm going in to bed."

He took two steps forward, which brought his face close to mine. "I'm a mite tired for games myself. Be a friend to yourself, Wade, and cut out the monkey business. I'm going to get that girl."

"That's your job."

I started by him, and he caught my arm. He had a grip like a steel trap.

"Somebody," he said, "took Vicky Hustin out of Clarence Oldham's car at gunpoint. I've questioned Oldham for the better part of an hour. He co-operated. In fact, he was burned up at being the victim of such highhandedness."

"If somebody took Vicky, why aren't you out trying to find her?"

"In this darkness? With her knowing the hills as well as a wild creature?"

"I don't mean that. Maybe some of Rock Hustin's people have got her. You ought to be checking that. You might have the start of a hill vendetta on your hands, while you've been here worrying my mother."

"You know better than that, Wade," he said in a voice thin with control. "I know you're sweet on that girl. I know you inquired about her whereabouts at the hotel and a few more places. Then you disappeared, and you've been gone all day. Somehow or other you caught something I missed. You knew where she and Oldham had gone, and you waylaid them."

He glanced at my mother. "Evalina, your boy is in serious trouble this time. Acting as accessory after the fact in a murder is something that can send him a long ways up the river."

My mother trembled. Her hand caught my arm. "If you know anything, Wade, you'd better tell the sheriff."

"I don't know a thing. Why are you picking on me, Kirk?"

"I'm not picking on anybody! I just want that girl. There can't be a single doubt that she killed her husband. Whatever kind of rat he was, she's got to take what's coming to her."

"There is the chance she's innocent."

He made a noise in his throat. "She'll have the opportunity to prove it. But it looks pretty open and shut to me."

"You're not paid to render opinions, Kirk."

His face was white with anger. "You'd better tell me, Wade. Her only chance is to return and stand trial."

He was a man with a one-track mind. The whole thing would be over as soon as he got Vicky and brought her to trial. No other suspects. No other directions for his bulldog mind to travel.

I took my mother by the arm and started toward the house. "Maybe Oldham hid her himself and lied to you, Kirk."

"He's not the man to take that chance. Anyhow, he didn't know she was wanted until he charged into town to tell me about a kidnaping."

"Well, I wish I could help. Good night, Kirk."

I was almost at the veranda when he said, "Wait a minute, Wade!"

I stopped and looked back. He walked to my car, pulled a flashlight from his hip pocket, and flashed the light around inside the car. He reached into the glove compartment and pulled out a pint bottle half full of whisky. He pitched the whisky in his own car and walked toward us.

"Wade, you ought to know better than to carry around that non-taxed 'shine."

I read the glint of triumph in his eyes. It tensed my muscles. "You've probably got a jug of your own around some place, Kirk."

"But nobody's arresting me for it," he said.

"And you're arresting me?"

"I'm afraid I have to. As you said, I'm not paid to render opinions. It's my opinion that the county is wrong in trying to stay dry. But as long as we have that law, it's my job to enforce it."

He pulled a pair of handcuffs from a black leather case hooked to his belt. One of the bracelets snapped closed on my left wrist. A cry caught in my mother's throat.

Real pain showed on Hyder's face. "Evalina, I'm sorry. More sorry than you'll ever know. But I think he'd better spend the night in town."

My mother's face was pale and thin, in the cold moonlight. "Wade, she's no good. She's not worth it!"

"Take her advice," Hyder urged.

"I don't know a thing," I said.

"All right, then," Kirk said, giving the cuffs a tug that showed his anger. "Let's go."

"Kirk," my mother said. "I really think—"

"I'm sorry, Evalina," he said again. He had me in the car by that time and we swept around the rigid, shocked figure of the little gentlewoman whose life had been an attempted denial that the world is a violent place.

A few minutes later Kirk pulled up before the courthouse.

MAN - KILLER

He motioned me out of the car, sticking close behind me. "Inside," he ordered.

The empty building echoed our footsteps. The old-fashioned, milky globes hanging in the corridor spilled pale light over a floor as warped and wavy as a lake.

Kirk pushed me into the elevator ahead of him. The cage of iron grillwork groaned, wobbled, and bumped its guides to the third, and top, floor of the courthouse. This whole floor was given over to the jail.

When the empty cell yawned before me, I became so mad I couldn't speak. I wouldn't move, either, until he had pulled his gun and prodded me in.

"Now, Wade," he said mildly, "let's see how much help you can give her from in there!"

4

Early the next morning, Josh Loudermilk, Kirk's fat deputy, brought my breakfast of flapjacks, grits, and sausage.

"Kirk come down yet?"

Josh grunted a negative. He picked his teeth and watched me eat. He was a big man, with a face that flowed over his collar and a stomach that repeated the process over his belt.

Finally, he stretched, yawned, and deigned to tell me, "Your mother is in his office waiting for him."

He carried the tin eating utensils out of the cell. An hour passed before he returned. "Kirk's here now. Come on."

Josh unlocked the cell, and I followed him downstairs to Kirk's office. My mother rose from a chair at the side of the desk. She looked as if she hadn't slept much. "I'm afraid I haven't convinced Kirk that you were telling the truth last night, Wade."

Kirk was behind his desk, leaning back in his swivel chair. He looked at me and said nothing. Josh Loudermilk closed the door and sat down.

Evalina turned to face Kirk. "Surely you'll give Wade a chance? You'll go through with the test?"

"What test?" I asked.

"Since it was Mr. Oldham the girl was with," my mother said, "I've insisted on Kirk bringing him over here for purposes of identification."

"Oldham said the man was screened by brush," Kirk said.

"You've told me that," Evalina said with a nod. "But Mr.

26

Oldham heard the man's voice. Won't that be sufficient? I'm positive he'll say to you it wasn't Wade's voice."

I lighted a cigarette, watching Kirk's face. His eyes were bland, but something in them made me uneasy. "All right, Evalina, we'll se what Oldham has to say."

Kirk picked up the phone and called the hotel. He asked the girl on the switchboard if she knew whether or not Mr. Oldham was awake yet. It seemed Clarence Oldham was in the coffee shop having breakfast. Four or five minutes later Kirk was talking with him.

Kirk hung up. "He'll come down." He looked at me with that hound-on-the-hot-trail gleam in his eyes. He had something up his sleeve, and I wasn't sure I would get any amusement out of the trick.

While we waited for Oldham, Evalina chatted with Kirk about the church circle to which she and Mrs. Hyder belonged. The drawn lines about her mouth were an indication of her inner humiliation as she sat in a sheriff's office pleading for a son under suspicion of having helped a hill girl avoid arrest as a murderess.

Finally a knock sounded on the door. Josh Loudermilk, emitting wheezing grunts, got to his feet. He crossed the office, opened the door, and Clarence Oldham came into the room.

Oldham said good morning all around and shook hands with Evalina when Kirk introduced them. Oldham's nod to me was frigid. I'd met him at the hotel, and he'd seen Vicky and me together a few times.

Oldham's brisk, quick movements, the intent flashing of his cold eyes behind black-rimmed glasses, brought a change to the office. He exuded efficiency, and you felt as if you needed to get on your toes and get going in his presence. Even Josh felt the change and shuffled faster than usual to push out a chair for Oldham.

"Reason I asked you to come down," Kirk said, "is because I think this is the man who kidnapped Mrs. Hustin."

Oldham looked at me, gave me a second nod which meant nothing, except that he acknowledged Kirk's statement.

"Now yesterday," Kirk said, "you stated the man was screened by brush."

"Correct."

"You saw nothing of him?"

"Nothing more than you'd expect."

"But the man spoke to you?"

"Several times."

"And you'd recognize the voice?"

"Most definitely, should I hear it again."

Kirk stood up. He motioned Josh over with a toss of his head. He whispered into the fat deputy's ear. Josh, glancing at me, nodded, grinned, and went out.

"You said the kidnaper was about a hundred yards away from you," Kirk said to Oldham.

"Right."

"Let's go outside," Kirk said.

Oldham, Kirk, my mother and I walked outside and got in Kirk's muddy sedan.

Kirk drove a block east, turned, and stopped at a large vacant lot. We got out of the car.

Kirk said, "Mr. Oldham, what was one of the things the man said?"

Oldham's eyes glinted. "He said, 'You take one step and I'll break your knees with rifle slugs.'"

28

Hyder glanced across the field. "Wade and I will walk over there a little way. You can turn your back or close your eyes or watch him if you like, and I'll have Wade repeat the sentence."

I felt needles of sweat on my brow. "I'm not sure I want to."

"You'll do it," Kirk said, "unless you've been lying." He jerked his thumb. I drew in a breath and walked across the field, Kirk behind me.

"Okay, Mr. Oldham?" Kirk called.

"Ready."

"Say it," Kirk said.

I looked at him, then at Oldham and the small, taut figure of Evalina at the edge of the field. Then I yelled, "You take one step and I'll break your knees with rifle slugs."

"Again in a higher voice," Kirk ordered.

I repeated the sentence; then a third time in a lower voice.

We walked back to the edge of the field. Evalina bit her lower lip and seemed unable to take her eyes away from Oldham's face. I patted her shoulder.

"Well?" Kirk asked.

Oldham looked me up and down. "It wasn't the voice," he said.

Evalina let out a breath that was almost a sob. "You see, Kirk . . ."

The arrival of Josh Loudermilk in a rattling coupe drew out attention. Josh banged the coupe's door shut when he got out. He grinned and winked at Kirk and handed him a small paper bag.

Kirk gave me a long glance; then he turned to Clarence

Oldham. "There's an old hill trick, Mr. Oldham," Kirk said, "when a man wants to disguise his voice."

Kirk opened the paper bag and poured gravel in his hand. "It's clean, Wade. Take a mouthful."

A constriction formed in my throat. The silence seemed sudden and heavy; then it was broken by a cicada, high in a tree, making a sound like a high-speed saw touching metal.

They were looking at me, waiting. A smile touched the corners of Kirk's thin-lipped mouth.

I held out my left hand. Kirk poured it full of gravel. I raised my hand to my mouth and took a mouthful of the gravel.

At Kirk's nod, I walked ahead of him into the field again. My pulse was heavy and thick. I studied the line of trees on the far side of the field. A fool's play. Even if I made cover and lost myself in the brush beyond the creek I knew was over there, Kirk would have the area blanketed in a matter of minutes.

"That's far enough, Wade," Kirk said.

I stopped.

"Say your piece."

I looked across the stretch between me and Oldham. I said the piece three times in different pitches of voice.

Kirk motioned me back toward Oldham. We again became a single group.

"Well?" Kirk said.

"He most definitely," Oldham said, "is not the man."

I heard the intake of my own breath. I glanced at Kirk. He looked as if somebody had hit him across the head with a billy.

Then I met Oldham's gaze, and I knew he was lying. I

30

didn't know why. I knew it wasn't because he wanted to see me have Vicky.

"Now, Kirk," Evalina said, "don't you owe us an apology for jailing Wade all night?"

"I guess I do," Kirk said, but his tone didn't imply such. He glanced at Josh as if anxious to tell the deputy something.

"You've had Calhoun in jail all night?" Oldham asked. "He hasn't changed clothes since yesterday?"

Kirk nodded. "Not that I know of."

"Then Calhoun couldn't have been the man in the brush. That man was wearing a blue shirt. That much I could see, impressions of blue mingled with the vivid green of the brush."

"You never mentioned a blue shirt before," Kirk said in an unwilling tone.

"You didn't ask me," Oldham said with a smile. "Sorry I couldn't help you."

"Not half as sorry as I am."

The two men shook hands and then Oldham walked away. I took Evalina by the arm and moved off behind him. I figured if Kirk had anything more to say he would call me back.

He let me go, probably thinking it would be best to give me rope and keep an eye on me, now that his theory about the kidnaping had been knocked apart.

When we arrived home my mother went straight to the kitchen, I went down the narrow hall to the small bedroom where the gardener had once slept. I was going to get out clean things and head for the bath. First, however, I took off my tan shirt and stood looking at it.

It struck me that Oldham's lie about the blue shirt had served a double purpose. It had helped to make his statement

to Kirk stick. And, equally important, it had removed any doubt from my mind that he had lied for me the first time, in the matter of voice identification. It meant he was positive I was the man who'd taken Vicky, and he wanted me to know it.

I followed the trend of thought. In crossing up Kirk Hyder, Oldham hadn't been motivated by any desire to help me out. I believe he would, on the contrary, have received a sardonic pleasure from hurting me if he could. Even without the explosive factor of Vicky, Oldham and I would have by mere contact aroused mutual, unspoken antagonism.

Now that Vicky was free without entangling him, he had given me the go-ahead sign to keep her free. He would play ball only so long as I was useful. He wanted her freedom as much as Kirk Hyder wanted her captivity.

Neither of them wanted anything good to happen to me.

5

As soon as we'd finished eating lunch, Evalina gave her mouth a dainty touch with her napkin, laid the cloth beside her plate, and folded her hands on the table. "Wade, you mustn't go back to her."

"I thought I went through all that with Kirk Hyder."

"Kirk wasn't there to watch Mr. Oldham's face during the identification. Perhaps Kirk wouldn't have seen anything anyway—it's such an inscrutable face. A woman senses those things, Wade. Mr. Oldham has heard your voice before."

"He should have told Kirk." I dropped my napkin on the table and started to get up.

"No! Sit down, Wade!" A new quality was in her voice, nothing of harshness, but a sibilance that caused me to think that silk, in its way, is stronger than steel. "You're going to hear me out, Wade!"

She waited until I was sitting again. She looked at her knuckles, white and work-worn, on the table. "For many years, Wade, I've been aware of your shortcomings. Do you know what's kept me going these past years? Not the short-comings, oh, no! There were times when I wanted to quit, go back to my father's house. Times when there were too many creditors to face, too many problems for one person to solve. I was unequipped from birth for these past years, Wade, but I saw them through. Pride helped. Perhaps it's a strange, perverse pride, but it helped.

"Yet pride alone was not enough. You were the reason, Wade. The thought that one day you would more than fill your father's shoes and recover much of what has been lost. This was our home. This was where we belonged.

"I told myself your shortcomings were only temporary, that as you grew older you would learn to channel your energies properly. This was what kept me going. I could make my mind and body immune to the present as long as there was hope for the future."

She stopped speaking as if she had run out of breath.

I looked away from the burning intensity of her eyes. I had no wish to hurt her. I knew she was wrong. It wasn't hope for the future that had kept her going. It was hope that the past could be brought to life again.

She was trying to read my face. She was clutching the edge of the table and leaning toward me. "You're picturing in your mind what you think is a noble thing," Evalina said. "You'll save this snip of mountain trash, this ex-wife of a criminal, this murderess. But have you considered what it will be like? You'll have to have money to live. You'll never dare let people know who you are, who she is, even if you succeed in getting her away. You'll have to run. You'll have to live in hiding. You'll one day begin to think of what might have been. You'll grow to hate her and wish you were rid of her."

I sat without moving.

"I haven't dissuaded you, have I, Wade?"

"I wish you wouldn't try. I wish you could just accept it as something that has to be. Learn to think of yourself a little more, live for yourself. You have a future, too. You've done wrong in wrapping up your future in another person."

"Why, Wade?" she cried. "Why do you insist on plunging ahead?"

"Because I know I'm right," I said truthfully. "And I know she's right. I know her too well to believe she's guilty."

"But do you know what she would do in a single moment of rage, of loss of self-control?"

"She learned self-control a long time ago. She doesn't react like an animal. She's worked and struggled too hard, she was too near her divorce, her freedom, to throw it away in a single moment."

"But you can't be *sure!* What you say may be true, but there is always the slim chance that you're wrong."

"I'll have to take that chance."

Evalina closed her eyes. Her head dropped. I reached the table and took her hand. It was icy.

"There is a choice you can make," I said. "We shouldn' be fighting. We belong on the same team."

Her breathing sounded stifled. "Give me a moment. A chance to realize what I should have known before. You're a man now. There comes a time to every man when he must stand alone."

I stood up and pushed the hair back from her forehead with its fine, tired lines. "I'll get in touch with you. I'll send you money. As long as she stays out of his hands, Kirk Hyder will keep working on the case. Theres a fair chance he might find the real murderer, and we can return."

"Do you have any money?"

"A little. Enough."

"When do you leave?"

"Tonight."

"You meet her then?"

"Yes," I said, "right after dark at the old Stillman place."

"Take real good care of yourself, Wade."

"I will. That's a promise."

She laid her face on her arms. I put my hand on her shoulder. There was a tearing sensation in my throat. I would have given an arm to have taken on myself what she was feeling.

I turned and quietly left the room.

When I went outside, I saw Josh Loudermilk's dusty coupe standing in the driveway. Josh was lounging against the fender, picking his teeth with a sharpened goose quill. He removed his toothpick and grinned at me. "Kirk being bush hunting her out in the hills, he told me to be friendly with you today, Wade."

"How friendly?"

"Thicker'n blood brothers. Closer to you than the skin on your back. Kirk ain't all the way convinced yet that you're lily clean. He figures I ought not to let you out of my sight. That being the case, we might as well make the best of it. Where we going?"

I shrugged. "To a movie, I guess."

"Shucks, I done seen the one playing in town."

"Then see it again."

Dusk was darkening the earth when Josh and I came out of the movie. A wind from the north was freshening, piling thunderheads over the distant mountains. It might be a rainy, dark, dreary night. A perfect night for running, with water from the skies to wash away the traces.

"Stinking picture, wasn't it?" Josh said. "Where do we eat?"

We ate in the Home Cooking Café, on the west side of the square. Spareribs, cabbage, corn bread. Washed down with bitter coffee.

36

MAN - KILLER

"I can see why the cook here ain't cooking at home no longer," Josh said. But he ate everything in sight and was asking the waitress for more coffee when I got up to leave.

He sighed with disappointment at the interruption and followed me out. Every slap-slap of his feet grated on my nerves. Time was running out. I had to get rid of him soon.

On the sidewalk, he grinned and picked his teeth. "Any plans for a big night, Wade?"

"You want a girl?"

"Subject ain't never far from my mind."

"We'll go to Timkin's Hollow."

The grin left his face. "Bad neighborhood."

"If you're afraid," I said, "you can stay here."

I got in my car, pulled off. His headlights flashed behind me. I drove to the east side of the square, and turned off on a side street. After half a dozen blocks, the street became a dirt lane. Another few blocks and it ran through a patch of woods.

I cut the ignition, letting the car buck to a stop in gear. Josh stopped behind me. I let the starter grind with the ignition off. Then I got out, a heavy five cell flashlight in my hand, standard equipment in cars that regularly traverse mountain roads.

I opened the hood and poked at the wiring. Curiosity drew Josh closer. "Maybe it's the carburetor," he offered.

I sighed, shook my head, turned—and hit him as hard as I could, using the flashlight for a club. I was aiming for his head, but he moved enough to catch the blow on his cheek. I plunged at him. He jerked back, trying to free his revolver from its holster. He used his free hand to grab my flashlight wrist, and I used mine to clutch his gun hand.

We wrestled back and forth for awhile. Then his hand jerked free, and a second later the gun went off.

I felt a tearing pain in my left temple, followed by the warmth of blood. I went sick, with the knowledge that I'd been shot; I stumbled backward. My senses tried to keep the world in focus and fight away the engulfing blackness.

Mixed with the roaring in my head was the distant sound of Josh's voice: "Wade, I didn't mean . . . You oughtta not have . . ."

I was falling. But I didn't know when I struck.

6

WHEN I came to I was in Josh's coupe and we were parked before a large white house.

I studied the pale outlines of the house in the glow of the street lamp. I realized it was Doc Braddock's place. Josh, I decided, had wasted no time getting me over here, no doubt frantic with the thought that I might be dying on his hands.

In a way, I wished I could.

I touched my left temple. It was still oozing blood, but not much. The bullet from Josh's gun had clipped a few hairs on my temple and ruptured a small blood vessel, making the wound look messy as death, but it hadn't touched bone. I was still living to prove that.

For the moment, I was free of Josh. He was up there in Doc Braddock's house, and if Braddock wasn't home, they'd be phoning all over town for him right now.

I had fought Josh, risked my life, for freedom to get to Vicky. Now I had that freedom, but I couldn't take advantage of it. My body was too weak. In his haste, Josh had left the keys in the ignition, but all I could do was touch them. Then I had to rest a few seconds.

I gripped the steering wheel and dragged myself across the seat. The effort drained me. I laid my head on the wheel. My stomach was jerking and I had to fight for breath.

I finally pulled my body up straight. Just then Braddock's porch light flashed on. I turned my head toward the light. It hurt my eyeballs. Indistinctly, I saw Josh on the porch.

He was coming back to the car. He must have located Braddock.

It was the jolt I needed. My hand found the keys. I got the ignition on, but I couldn't find the starter. My fingers moved over the dashboard I mashed a button or two. Nothing happened.

Finally I brought my foot down on the accelerator. The starter gave a short, quick gruff and the car lurched. Out of the corner of my eye I was watching Josh's bulk with the porch light behind it. He stopped. Then he yelled and came running.

I threw in the clutch, mashed the accelerator down. The starter ground, and the motor came to sudden, surging life.

Josh threw himself at the coupe. I let the clutch go. The car got away so fast you could smell rubber burning. Mingled with the scream of tortured rubber was Josh's shouted curse.

The acceleration threw me against the back of the seat. My weight threw the wheel to one side, and the coupe swayed. A light pole rushed at me. I fought the wheel back and the light pole shot past.

I righted the coupe and got it straightened out. I glanced in the rear-view mirror. Josh was standing in the middle of the street, pulling his gun. He didn't fire. Maybe his narrow brush with killing tonight had made him allergic to guns. Maybe he just didn't want to chance me piling up his car.

The thought of the gun, however, kept an expectant knot of muscle in my back until I turned a corner.

The coupe wanted an experienced jockey. It was equipped with dual carburetors and a high-speed rear end, and it was sensitive to every touch of the wheel and accelerator. It expressed a constant challenge to my mastery.

MAN - KILLER

I began to get the feel of the coupe as I rolled it along the highway. The lights of Big Hominy dropped behind, and air, chilled with altitude and darkness, rushed through the window beside me. My head began to clear, and I was feeling pretty good by the time I swung off the macadam onto the fir-and-brush-shadowed dirt road that crawled toward the spine of the mountain. The brush slapped at the car. I fought the ruts, slowing enough so the curves wouldn't pitch me into a tree.

The coupe ate up the remaining miles of mountain. The road petered out; and there was the spot where I'd parked my own car the day before.

I stopped the coupe and got out. Above me in the small clearing, the old Stillman house squatted dark and silent.

The exertion of walking to the house left me breathing hard. The door was open. I stood in the dark frame, getting my breath back.

"Vicky?" My voice sounded thin against the rising night wind that troubled the woods.

Was she hiding? Could she have gone to sleep? If she were hiding outside, she would have seen me arrive. She wouldn't have recognized the coupe, but she would have recognized me as I crossed the clearing.

The cabin was a musty black hole. I bumped into the rickety table. I groped for the lantern, almost knocked it to the floor, caught it, and got it lighted.

"Vicky!"

I carried the lantern to the cabin door, holding it so I was plainly visible. I touched my dry lips with my tongue and yelled her name. Then I went out in the clearing and yelled it two or three more times.

MAN - KILLER

I stood outside the cabin more than long enough for her to call back and walk toward me and the light in my hands.

I fought a feeling of empty helplessness. I went back in the cabin and set the lantern on the hand-hewn table.

The stove was giving off heat. I opened one of the rusty eyes and looked at the way a couple of sticks were burning. All the bark hadn't caught yet. I'd seen enough wood fires to know the sticks hadn't been in the stove longer than ten or fifteen minutes. Twenty minutes at the most. She couldn't have gone far . . . if she had been the last one to feed the fire.

A slight sound in the doorway caused me to drop the stove eye and spin about. With my nerves already jangled and the night wind moaning about the cabin, I stopped breathing at the sight of the face. A grotesque face, scarred and evil.

It was the face of Hap McCall, and it made you realize that miracles do happen; it was a miracle that Vicky had been sired by this man.

Hap was tall, bony, stooped, his shoulders rounded to make him look hollow-chested and weak. He was anything but weak. He could hunt or fish three days at a time without much sleep or food, in any kind of weather, over any terrain. He had the physical tenacity of a briar tree growing out of rocky soil. The auto crash, which had so disfigured the left side of his face, would have killed some men. Hap had recovered with not as much trained medical help as some people give a raw throat.

"Looking for Victorina, ain't you?" The grin became a leer on the unpleasant mask of his face.

The start he'd given me passed. I slid the stove eye in place.

My bloody face seemed to afford him pleasure. Hap's kind had always hated people like the Calhouns.

Hap took two steps into the cabin. The lantern put a cold glow in his one good eye.

"Had a little trouble getting here to see her, appears like," he said. "Got yourself all banged up just so's you could come and look at the place where she ain't."

"Do you know where she is?"

"I reckon she's on her way to town."

I stared at him.

"On her way to the gas chamber," he added.

I was careful to grip the edge of the table and keep it between us. Even an animal protected his own; Hap merely sounded pleased that she was finished. There were no grounds for understanding Hap. No grounds for anything except hating.

"If you know what happened up here, Hap, spill it."

He just grinned. On his scarred face, it was a grimace.

"She left with Kirk Hyder?" I asked.

He nodded.

I heard my words come thick and slow. "Did you turn her in, Hap?"

Without full consciousness of what I was doing, I had moved around the table.

A vein began to throb in his right temple. "You need breaking, Calhoun," he snarled. "Same as she's always needed breaking. Too good for her own kind, despising the house that fed her, working in the fancy hotel and slipping goodies in to the old lady behind my back. Afraid of me and hating me. By hell, the likes of that ain't no daughter of mine!"

MAN-KILLER

He began to lose himself in a fine rage. He cursed, threatened, and boasted; then he worked up to his story. "I seen it all. I seen car lights on the road across the mountain. Then Kirk Hyder ran the car on the edge of the road, got out, and walked across the ridge. He came straight over here, just like somebody had drawed him a map. The cabin was dark, but there was a taint of wood smoke on the air.

"Kirk watched the place for a little while. Then he worked his way down to the cabin. I lost him a time or two in the shadows. Then I heard her scream. She sounded like an old woman crying out in the middle of a nightmare.

"Kirk came out of the cabin with her. She stumbled across the ridge with him. A few minutes later I follered. I seen the car lights flash up. Kirk drove to a turn-around in the road and headed back toward town."

He grinned wetly, looking at my face to see how I was taking it.

"Had it all planned, didn't you, Calhoun? But you was too late. You didn't miss them by much. Fact is, if you took the county road, you passed them."

With a strange, detached calm, I put it together in my mind. There was a blank spot or two. For example, I didn't know how Hap had located her. Maybe in his hill wanderings he'd passed the cabin and seen her. Maybe he'd heard the crack of my rifle when I'd put the furrow in the metal of Oldam's car.

The blank spots could be filled in later. The only thought my mind could hold was the certainty that after Hap had located her, he had notified Kirk Hyder and then watched the results like a skulking hill varmint.

I hit him in the face and knocked him against the cabin

44

wall. Right away I knew it was a mistake. My head hurt blindingly, and the effort drained my strength. Wiry and tough, Hap had a good chance of tearing me in two in my present condition.

He made a cackling noise of glee, braced himself against the wall, and came at me. I had one more punch left. I used it, and was strong enough to send him back to the wall.

Some of the edge was knocked from his eagerness, but none from his determination.

"You damn Calhoun," he said softly. "I'm going to kill you. Before you die, I want you to know the killing was a pleasure."

He wiped a fleck of blood from his lips, not taking his eye from me. He put his hand in the pocket of his greasy overalls. He pulled out a switchblade knife and it snicked open with a little metallic sound.

My throat felt parched. I regretted having lost my head and having started open trouble. But I'd never let him see it. I'd die before I'd admit it to him.

He sprang, and I moved back. The knife glinted. I bumped against the stove. There was no further retreat.

I twisted my head, and the knife missed my face by inches.

He grunted; he was off balance. When he turned, he ran into the stick of stovewood I'd grabbed.

He staggered, amazement and shock on his face. I hit him again on the side of the head. His knees buckled. His face displayed a desperate inner effort to retain consciousness. Even as he fell, he tried to throw the knife. It fell at my feet.

I tapped him a final time with the stovewood. I hit him lightly, not because I particularly wanted to be lenient, but because it was all that was necessary. His collapse jarred the cabin.

I reached down and picked up his knife. It was a wicked weapon, with a long, upcurving blade. I put the blade on the floor, stepped on it, and jerked the handle.

Before I walked from the cabin, I laid the pieces of broken knife at Hap's fingertips.

7

I DROVE back to town, went around the square, and saw lights burning in the courthouse. I parked Josh's coupe and went into the building.

Hearing my footsteps, Josh came to the door of Kirk's office. Josh stared at me, witless. Then his face darkened. He hitched his pants and swaggered toward me, his chin thrust out.

He might have saved himself the trouble, because he didn't bluff me. He didn't work at the job of deputy because he was tough. He worked because the job was easy most of the time, added to his prestige, and enabled him to escape manual labor.

I pitched him the keys of his car. "Your crate's outside," I said, "none the worse for wear."

He looked at the keys and rubbed his cheek where I'd bruised it with the flashlight. Then he looked at the furrow on my scalp and shrugged as if the score were even in his mind.

"You sure gave me a start, Wade. First I'm certain I killed you. Then you go busting off from the doctor's that way. Now you come ankling back, looking like you got the short end of the deal."

I would go along with that too. "I guess you're right," I admitted.

"I better let the state boys know I got my car back. I picked up your crate—it's parked behind the courthouse."

I followed him into the office. He pulled his goose-quill toothpick from his pocket, wiped it between his fingers, and explored a frontal cavity. "Didn't do you no good, going up there."

"No," I said. "You've seen Kirk, then?"

"Helped him question the girl when he brought her back. Just this minute finished. He's taken her upstairs."

I turned and started from the office. Josh moved around in front of me.

"Now, Wade, you know you can't go up there. Ain't visiting hours. Your head looks too bad to be running around any more. Why don't you take it home and put it to bed?"

"Josh, a lot of starch has been wrung out of me, and I'm not trying to start anything, but I want to go up and let her know I tried."

He shook his head.

"You can stretch a point that much," I said.

"Nope. Kirk's already sore as a hornet-stung bear dog. She didn't help matters none. Got under Kirk's skin, the way she sat and stared right through him when he was trying to talk to her. Wouldn't say nothing. Wouldn't show nothing. Just sat there and stared, like people was something she wouldn't even spit on.

"Kirk kept telling her he would help her if he could, if she would tell him how she'd killed Rock Hustin. Hell, if she copped a plea they wouldn't execute her. Kirk tried to explain that. He tried to show her how she'd spook a jury for certain, acting the way she was, not the least bit sorry or humble.

"Kirk finally got out of patience and took her upstairs. Now if I let you go up there and start a ruckus, Kirk's going to be bad to work for the next couple of weeks."

He was telling me how remorseless she was, how big a

fool I was for not going on home and going to bed. I knew
he was wrong. In my short stretch of Korean service, I'd
heard of POW's who had an affliction similar to hers. They'd
called it the five-hundred-mile stare. A man witnessed all
the horrors his mind could hold; then he walked over and
sat down and stared. At nothing. He simply stared, and grew
thinner and weaker. Most of them had died.

I dodged around Josh and reached the gloomy corridor.
He cursed and came after me. I reached the staircase ahead
of him and started up. The passage was dark, the stairs
uneven, each scooped out by the passing of countless feet
over many years.

Josh started up behind me with the silence of a freight en-
gine coupling cars. He yelled my name twice; then he saved
his breath.

My knees almost buckled on the second floor. A lighter,
faster man than Josh could have caught me easily; but from
the sounds issuing from the stairwell, I seemed to have gained
a little on him.

The entry to the stairway going on up was a dozen feet
away. I hesitated only long enough to listen for sounds of
the elevator bumping its way down. I didn't hear it. Kirk
must still be up there.

I reached the third floor . . .

The floor of steel and caged space. A couple of overhead
lights, snug against the ceiling in small, steel-mesh cases, never
permitted full darkness. I drew up short. The elevator was
bumping, taking Kirk down.

I ran down the corridor to the steel-barred door that shut
off the women's section. It was around a short ell and the
lighting was very dim.

MAN - KILLER

The individual cells were a dozen or more feet beyond the section door. I saw her. She was in the third cell, the only one occupied. She was a slender shadow, and the dim light etched her as she stood on the hard, low bunk bolted to the far wall.

She had knotted her stockings together to give her the length of rope she needed. She'd fastened one end of the rope with a slipknot to an overhead steampipe. She was ready to knot the other end about her throat. Then she would step from the bunk and it would all seem to be over. She'd be free of the final cage in a caged life. She'd have found one way out.

But that way can never be the right way. It solves nothing. It only removes you from every hope of solving anything, takes you forever from a change of fortune that tomorrow or next week might give your life a completely different color.

I knew.

This way she was trying had been my father's way—and within a year of his death rich deposits of feldspar had been discovered on lands manipulated for the railroad that never came. He might have had a chance to save at least a remnant of the land, a remnant that would have squared him, but he had thrown the chance away in a terrible, pitiful moment when he denied the future.

My mind was aghast with the futility of such an act. My lips began screaming her name.

I yelled loud enough to wake the whole damn town, and I rattled and beat the bars until it seemed the whole building should be shaking with the vibration.

The commotion shocked her to sudden immobility. She

stood looking at me and I kept yelling. I don't know what I said. Her name. Words. Anything to hold her attention.

Kirk heard and returned to the third floor. Josh arrived also. They rushed up behind me, Kirk with my name angrily on his lips. He was ready to give me a hiding down, but he saw what I had seen, and he jerked out his keys.

He opened the first door. He seemed to me to be moving much too slowly. But I didn't crowd him or get in his way. With a squeal of steel hinges that needed oiling, the second door swung.

Vicky didn't move until we were in her cell. Then she stepped down from the bunk, her face like a beautiful painting done by an artist who has failed to breathe life into his creation.

She looked at us as if she couldn't believe we were there. She moved her head slowly to give the dangling stocking a long look. Then something snapped inside of her. She covered her face with her hands. A tremor shook her body. A low, hoarse cry came from her lips.

She was unresisting as I pushed her onto the bunk and covered her with a blanket. She was sobbing as no human being should.

I glanced over my shoulder at Kirk.

His face was gray. "Josh is gone to bring the doc over." He touched his lips with his tongue. "Wade, I'm sorry."

An apology from Kirk was unusual. I knew what it cost. I sensed his meaning, too. He was a hunter, but he despised those who hunted and needlessly tortured their prey.

"Wade," he said, "watch after her until the doc arrives."

He left the cell quickly, leaving me alone with her.

When I turned back to Vicky, she was looking at me, her

51

eyes dilated until they were like drops of ink in her pale face. Her sobs had subsided until they were only an occasional convulsive shuddering of her body.

I wiped the fine, cold sweat from her forehead. She said weakly, "Don't worry, Wade. I won't try it again. I must have been crazy."

"Don't talk about it, Vicky."

She closed her eyes and lay silent for a few seconds. The overhead light glinted on the tear streaks on her cheeks.

"Why'd you do it, Wade?"

"Do what?"

"Tell her."

"I don't get it."

"You told your mother where I was to meet you. She told Kirk."

The hairs at the back of my neck began to feel like needles pricking the skin. A rigidity settled in my arms and legs. For a second, I had the feeling that I couldn't move if I tried.

Vicky looked at my face; then she sat up on the bunk quickly. She caught my hand and pressed it tightly against her cheek.

"Wade, you mustn't blame her!"

"She tricked me."

"She was fighting to keep her world intact, Wade."

"She hit low, even if she is my mother."

"I'd have done the same—for our son. Would you want him to try and understand?"

"She's the cause of your being caught, brought to this place. Yet you still speak this way of her."

Vicky glanced away. "It's not because I'm good, Wade. I don't want you messing up your life completely. I told you after you stopped Oldham's car. It's no good. You'll destroy yourself."

I reached out, took her chin in my hand, and forced her face in the direction of mine, until our eyes met.

"No," I said, speaking with slow care, "this is the one chance I've got to find myself. I don't know exactly what's happened to me, but I'm not the same Wade Calhoun I was last week or even two days ago. Success or failure never meant much to me in the past. I was supposed to be the end product of a family sunken in decay. The past was so big and tangled up that it obscured the future.

"Now I've learned something. The past is big only when you put small meaning in your life. Now success means everything—it's the future."

"Crazy Wade," she said, a fresh warmth in her voice. "You choose a time like this to discover a future?"

"It happens that way sometimes."

"I could listen to you long enough and almost think there might be a future."

"There will be! No one can stop me now, Vicky. No one except you."

Again she glanced at the dangling stockings.

"Don't hate yourself for it," I said. "Be as kind to yourself as you would to another person in your place. Forgive yourself—and try to believe, Vicky!"

She laid her cheek against mine and she was crying again. But it was different this time. She said softly, "I'll believe, Wade."

I knew she would, and the sense of failure was no longer so acute.

Footsteps approached the cell. Kirk and Doctor Braddock

came in. Braddock checked her pulse and heart. He took a needle from his bag. She didn't flinch when he swabbed a spot on her arm and jabbed her. She was looking at me when the hypo took effect. Her eyes glazed and then closed and she was asleep.

Kirk stirred heavily; Braddock snapped his bag closed and stood up.

"Shock," Braddock said. "She'll probably be okay when she wakes. Better have the night deputy look in on her now and then."

We went downstairs. Braddock, when we were in Kirk's office, pointed to a chair. "Sit down, Wade."

I sat. Braddock opened his bag again. He swabbed the gash on my temple, bandaged it, and left.

Kirk sat on the edge of his desk, facing me. "You've tried to hamstring the law and run off with a deputy's car, Wade. Both jailable offenses. But you brought the car back, and I got her. That's the important thing. So I'm going to let you go with a final warning. Stay out of it! Leave my case against her alone or I'll make you curse the day you ever set eyes on her."

I didn't feel like arguing. "You certainly seem to have drawn to a flush and filled it," I said.

I left the courthouse, crossed the square, and entered the Old Homestead Hotel. The elderly night clerk showed me to a room on the second floor. I got my shoes off, shucked my pants and shirt and draped them on the back of a chair.

I made it to the bed. Then I collapsed.

8

WHEN I went downstairs the next morning the day clerk was on duty. He was a thin young man, uncomfortable as he motioned me over. I'd slept off a couple of binges in the Old Homestead.

"I don't believe you paid in advance, Mr. Calhoun."

I paid him for the night's lodgings.

He relaxed. "A gentleman over there to see you."

I turned. Clarence Oldham was sitting across the musty-smelling lobby. He rose and walked toward me.

"Good morning, Calhoun." His face was without expression. His manner was unhurried, though the brisk aura he wore made you feel that things were about to happen. Things he might aloofly manipulate and control.

"How are you, Oldham?"

He shrugged. "Had breakfast?"

"Not yet."

"I'll join you in coffee, if you don't mind."

"Not at all."

We walked out of the hotel and went to the Home Cooking. It was about nine thirty and the place was almost deserted, peopled by a waitress and two customers at the counter. Oldham and I took a table in the corner. The waitress came out of her slouch and bounced over.

I ordered breakfast and Oldham asked for coffee. The waitress bustled about, filling our water glasses, bringing silverware, and Oldham remained silent until she started us with coffee and retired out of earshot.

Then he said coldly, "You failed, Calhoun. I thought I made it quite clear to you yesterday that I knew you'd taken Vicky from my car."

"You did. The lie about the clothes I was wearing clinched it for me."

He sipped his coffee. "Your thought processes seemed rapid enough to me. I knew you'd realize what I was doing."

"Just what were you doing, Oldham?"

"Leaving her free until something turned up in her favor. This country sheriff will quit now and sit back until time for the trial. He's got her and he's got his case. As long as she was free he had to keep working, looking. There was a chance he would stumble onto something, or that you would. You're the one I was counting on. In any event, I was quite willing to play along with you, although I won't forget that you pointed the wrong end of a gun at me."

"I don't want trouble, Oldham. You know why I used the gun."

"There'll be no trouble between us—as long as she's in danger. Trouble would only destroy any remaining chance she might have."

"Once she's free?"

He looked at me silently for a moment. "We'll cross that bridge when we come to it."

I rested my elbows on the table. "If I had reached her before Kirk Hyder did last night, I might have run away with her."

"I'd have found you," he said with no bravado.

"Who the hell are you, Oldham?"

"A Charlotte businessman on vacation. A man accustomed

56

to having things his way, buying what he wants, paying well for everything he gets. I want Vicky."

"She isn't for sale."

"I'm prepared to bid high."

"Not that high. You'd have to own Fort Knox."

"I think you misunderstand me, Calhoun. If she had placed a cash value on herself, do you think I'd want her? I can bid a great measure of respect, real affection, consideration, and kindness." He sat with his coffee cup held lightly, half raised to his lips. "There is, however, one thing cash might buy. Her freedom."

"It buys a lot of things."

"Kirk Hyder?"

"You might bribe Kirk Hyder," I said, "in a million years with the resources of the Treasury of the United States."

"I see. One of those. The deputy, Josh Loudermilk—is he smart enough to be of any assistance?"

"He might be."

"He could be bought?"

"I'm not sure about Josh. He's easy-going, disinclined to hard work. He'll look the other way when a hill man with a patch of farmed-out mountain makes a little run of 'shine to exchange for grits and beans. But if the hill man tried to organize the trade or do more than feed his kids, I think Josh would give him a lot of trouble."

We fell silent as the waitress put my bacon and eggs in front of me. Oldham ordered a second cup of coffee.

"Do some shopping, Calhoun," Oldham said. "I'll pay the bill."

"How high?"

"I'm looking for value, not a bargain. You can start counting in the low thousands."

He finished his second cup of coffee and stood up. His smile was bleak. "I know you won't attempt profiteering, Calhoun. Her safety is without price, but my money is intended for no other purpose."

He nodded his head in farewell and walked out of the café. I watched him through the window. He was headed for the courthouse.

I finished my breakfast without much appetite. I'll admit it—Oldham scared me. If a miracle did occur and she got out of that cell, how tough would he be to handle?

I doubted that his way would work. You hear talk of jurymen and judges being bought, and it happens. But setting out yourself to make it happen is something else again. The mountain people who vote and serve on juries have a characteristic way of viewing bribes. One mistaken attempt would result in the bribe offer being reported to Kirk Hyder.

Even if Oldham's way worked, the trial was bound to look bad. This didn't matter to him. He intended to take her away from here, to a place where the condemnation and resentment wouldn't matter. I wanted it better than that. I wanted the evidence against her shown up for what it was. I wanted truth to destroy the falsehood. Where do you start looking? How do you go about a thing like that?

I decided the best place to start with the knot was right at its nub. The victim. Rock Hustin.

I paid my check and walked out of the café. Evalina was waiting outside, so close to the door I almost bumped into her.

"Wade," she said, "I've been looking for you. You didn't

58

come home last night." She glanced away. "Kirk promised me he wouldn't tell you."

"He didn't."

"Wade, we can't talk here. I want to explain."

"I know why you did it, I think."

"You're not angry," she said, looking up into my face. "But I can see that I'm not getting through to you."

She stood there with the years crowding in on her and the soul-searching of a sleepless night haunting her and the incarceration of a girl who might go to the gas chamber on her conscience.

Tears came to her eyes. "Wade, you've changed."

I put my arm around her gently. "I'll get you home in a taxi. You're tired."

"Yes," she said, "so very tired. It's a relief to admit it." She glanced across the square at the courthouse. "Ask her to forgive me, Wade. It was something I felt I had to do. Tell her that the very act of doing it made me see things differently. The moment I did it, I began to wonder, to question myself as I never have before."

"She knows. She understands."

"Does she truly? I hope so, Wade. I see that she's changing our lives. It's something no one can stop. Do what you must, Wade. And I mean it sincerely this time. Free her. For her sake and yours—and lastly, for mine, to keep me from going to my grave with the mark of Judas on my soul."

She turned and started quickly away. I moved toward her. I reached her side as she reached the curb. She glanced up.

"Thanks, Mom."

She nodded, a faint smile touching her lips. Then she crossed the square, going toward the courthouse. She had conceded defeat with a grace rarely seen in the world today. From this day forward, she would accede to my decisions. Already adapting herself to the new status, she was on her way now, I suspected, to see Vicky.

The idlers on the street busied themselves in conversation as I turned to go. As I passed, they nodded to me as if they'd just seen me.

Rock Hustin was at Daley's Funeral Home, on a side street off the square. Daley's daughter, a slender blonde girl who was out of place in the silence and faint smell of embalming fluid, was on duty in the office.

I told her I'd like to see her father. In a few minutes I was talking with Henry Daley. The girl was discreetly busy elsewhere.

Henry was a slender, precise man with unruly, iron-gray hair. He gave the impression of absent-mindedness, preoccupation; but his wit was quick, and he was one of those rare people who place friendship beyond value. He had gone to college with my father, remaining a friend until the very end.

After we shook hands and he asked about my mother, he seated himself behind his desk, motioned me to a chair, and permitted himself a short chuckle. "You Calhouns never do anything halfway, do you, Wade?"

"I just don't believe she's guilty."

He rocked back in his swivel chair. "Suppose you knew, without a shadow of doubt, that she was guilty. What then?"

I knew I could be honest with Daley. "I don't think it would make too much difference. There are circumstances to consider."

"True. Frankly, I expected to have Rock as a customer a long time ago."

I studied Henry's face. Though Doc Braddock acted as pathologist when necessary, Daley augmented his undertaker's income with the office of country coroner. I wondered if my voice were going to sound faint. "Are you telling me you've discovered something which proves she's guilty?"

"I'm telling you that you haven't got a prayer of a chance, Wade. Kirk's got her boxed. Motive. Opportunity. He's certain to get an indictment. The odds are all against her when she comes to trial. It's going to be hard to get a neutral jury. You know how husband-killing is regarded in these hills. The evidence will carry a lot of weight—her fingerprints on the poker, her being at the scene of the crime at the approximate time of Rock's death. Are you certain you want to be involved in such a hopeless cause?"

I looked at him without saying anything.

"You'll ruin forever any remaining chances you may have personally in this town. People will never forget, Wade. The Calhoun name will have had it final hour.".

"I like you too much to see you wasting your breath, Daley."

"Fine. If you're hell bent on tilting against the windmills, then I'll offer you any assistance I can within the limits of my office."

9

THERE WAS a small cold room in the rear of the building. Two white lights glared overhead. On a table in the center of this room lay the body of Rock Hustin.

He was naked, his flesh in death giving the appearance of dough, his folded arms and barrel chest matted with a heavy growth of hair. The light was pitiless against his heavy jaw, sloping forehead, and beetling brows.

Daley closed the door behind us and we walked toward the dead man.

"Braddock will do an autopsy tonight," Henry said. "It'll make the record official. There's no doubt in our minds now that Hustin was killed by the head blow."

I swallowed my squeamishness and looked at the death wound. Rock had been hit hard above the right temple. The flesh was gray, torn, and puckered about the wound. The ruptured skin accented the sickening impression of indented bone. Below the wound, a ragged, deep scratch, ran down the side of Rock's face to his lower jaw bone.

I glanced at Henry. "What's the official explanation of the big scratch down the side of his face?"

"She raked him with the tip of the poker as he fell or after he was down." He looked at me and added, "Not necessarily my opinion. The official explanation. You asked for it."

My voice was harsh. "Use your imagination, Henry. Try to picture it as Kirk Hyder has it so nearly blocked out. She and Rock are in the fish cabin, facing each other. He threatens her, or lunges toward her. She picks up the poker and strikes, making the wound on his temple. Rock falls. She stands over him and deliberately draws the tip of the poker down the side of his face, making the scratch on his jaw. She's that calm and collected—cold-blooded. Still, in the next moment she's rushing from the cabin, so rattled she hasn't even thought of fingerprints on the poker. In the name of common sense, it's full of holes!"

Daley's eyes were shrewd as he looked at me. "You could be wrong about her, Wade."

His quiet words made me feel empty.

"She might have lied to you, Wade," he said. "Faced with sufficient reason, anyone might lie."

I shook my head. "I won't deny that, Henry. But she didn't lie to me about this."

"You sound very sure."

"I've got reasons. She knew she could level with me. A lie wouldn't help her. It would only hurt her chances by leaving me up a creek without a paddle."

I gave Rock's body a final glance. "Damn it, Henry, Rock was strong. He would have defended himself. You think he stood there and let a woman hit him?"

"If she moved fast enough, she could have hit him. It wouldn't be the first time a woman's strength has felled a man."

I tried to scorn Henry's words with a laugh. "She must have moved like chain lightning. She reached for the poker. She turned. She lifted the poker. She swung. I can't see it. Rock would have been on her the second she reached for the poker. And don't tell me he was afraid of the weapon. It would have taken a better weapon than that to have held him still."

"Such as?"

63

"A gun. If you said she was holding a gun on him, reached behind her and got the poker, it might tell better."

Daley smiled bleakly. "Don't go around repeating that. You might put ideas in Kirk's mind."

We left the room then and went back to Henry's office. Before he had a chance to sit down behind his desk, I said, "You accidentally leave the prelim report on your desk and enjoy the scenery from the window a few moments?"

"Could be." He shuffled papers on his desk. "I'll see if I'm needed in back."

I waited until he went out and closed the door. Alone in the office, I studied the report. It was skimpy. Time of death: between 9:00 and 11:00 P.M. the night of the tenth. Probable cause of death: cerebral hemorrhage following skull fracture. Weapon: probably steel rod, formerly used as a fireplace poker.

There was a little more about the location of Deaf Joyner's fish camp, brief information about Rock's next of kin, and a date for a complete autopsy.

Daley gave me ample time. When he returned, I was standing at the window smoking a cigarette.

"Thanks, Henry."

"I wish I could help, Wade."

"You have."

He moved behind the desk and sat down. "I wish I had your faith. Any of us might at some time swing a poker with enough provocation. She's no exception to the human race."

"To me," I said, "she is."

She was calm today. Her clothes were wrinkled and she

MAN - KILLER

wore no make-up. She'd never worn much make-up anyway, and her face was shiny clean and her hair neatly combed into a bun at the back of her neck.

Kirk wasn't around the courthouse and his second deputy hadn't felt inclined to argue about me seeing her. But I had to stay out beyond the second door, the corridor door, which left it and her cell door separating us. She stood at one door and I was at the other. We talked across the intervening distance.

"Can I get you anything, Vicky?"

"No, I'm okay."

"I would have been here earlier, but Oldham beat me over."

"Yes, he was here." Her face didn't tell me whether she'd been pleased to see Clarence or not. Then some animation came into her eyes. "Your mother was here too, Wade."

"I'm thankful for that."

"I am too. She's all right, Wade."

"How about her son?"

"Oh, he'll pass in a rush."

My throat felt too thick to keep it light. I guessed she felt the same way.

"Listen," I said, "I've been over to see Henry Daley. I saw the prelim report. All you need to account for is two hours of time. Maybe less. What time did you go to Deaf Joyner's place?"

"About midnight. I was alone in my room at the hotel all evening. I had a terrific headache, thinking about Rock being back and sending for me. I lay in the dark, trying to go to sleep. Finally, I couldn't stay in the room any longer. I had

65

to see Rock and tell him to leave me alone. My divorce was too near, and I wanted him to stay out of my life."

I was a juryman listening to that. I felt a tremor cross my shoulders.

I glanced around to make sure we still had privacy. "Anybody in your room? Some of the hotel help, maybe?"

"No, I was alone the whole time until I went out."

"Anyone see you leave?"

"Not that I know of."

"How'd you get from the hotel to Deaf Joyner's?"

"I put on some flat-heeled shoes and walked. It isn't far, cutting short of the ridge and down the old trail toward the lake."

"What time did you get there?"

"After midnight. I knocked and no one answered. Then I looked in the cabin. A small fire was in the fireplace. I thought he was out for a minute. I started to leave, but I'd made the trip and I didn't want it to be for nothing. So I stepped inside. It wasn't until I was in the cabin that I saw him . . . near the wall, his face bloody."

She choked, and had to swallow to keep on talking. "I wanted to bolt. Then I thought he needed help. I went over to him. I knew he was dead, then. I could tell by his eyes. I heard the noise outside, picked up the poker, and a few hundred years passed before I got out of there."

"Where was the poker when you picked it up?"

She frowned. "Funny, I don't remember. It might have been near Rock. I don't remember moving all the way to the fireplace."

"You might have?"

"Yes, I might."

"Rock mentioned trouble when he said he wanted to see you, didn't he?"

She nodded. "He didn't say what kind. Just sent word by a hill youngster that he had a tick in his hide—it was one of his favorite expressions—and wanted to see me."

"You don't know where he'd been or what he'd been doing since he left this part of the country?"

"No, Wade. I know only that I never wanted him to return."

I released the cell-door bars and wiped my palms with a handkerchief. "He ever mention Clarence Oldham? Or did Oldham ever mention Rock?"

"Rock didn't mention Clarence. I talked with Clarence some about my marriage, after we were well acquainted."

"Clarence bring up the subject or did you?"

"He did, come to think of it."

"As if he wanted information?"

Her face snapped up. "Why do you say that?"

"Just a wandering thought. Oldham showed up at the Stonewall Jackson Hotel right after reports began to drift around that Rock was back. I wondered if Rock's return, Oldham's appearance, and Oldham's quick interest in you, Rock's ex-wife, were all simply a matter of coincidence."

She tried to smile. "Clarence seemed to fancy me for myself alone."

"Subnormal if he didn't." I glanced at my wrist watch. Kirk's second deputy would be along to check up any minute now. "One more question. Have you told any of this to Kirk?"

"No. I was so low last night I wouldn't answer his questions. He hasn't talked to me much today."

"You scared him last night. He might not talk to you until tonight or tomorrow. Have you told anyone else, anyone at all, what you've told me?"

"No, Wade."

"Clarence?"

"He didn't talk about last night when he came up."

"Good." I heard the rattle and bump of the elevator ascending. The sound died out. Then I heard someone coming down the corridor.

I said in a swift, harsh whisper, "I haven't time to explain, Vicky. You'll have to obey me blindly."

"What must I do, Wade?"

"Say nothing. No matter how much you're questioned, tell Kirk nothing. Repeat your name, age, and address. Then stare holes through him. I'll tell you what to say when the time comes."

"You've thought of something?"

"A possible way out." I hesitated. She had been so long without hope. "In a matter of hours, Vicky, it may all be over—like a bad dream."

10

I DROVE up the winding driveway to the Stonewall Jackson and permitted my eyesore of a jalopy to infect the parking area. An attendant hurried over. "Never mind," I said. "The boat will be among its richer relatives only a short while."

I went up the walk that bisected the terraced lawn. On the plateau below, Big Hominy was a toy town, clean and quaint from this distance. Beyond the hotel was the backdrop of sky and towering, hazed-over mountains.

Clarence Oldham was waiting for me in the lobby. He rose from a deep club chair and came over to greet me.

"You sounded urgent on the phone, Calhoun."

"I feel that way," I said. "Where can we talk?"

"My room."

We rode the elevator to the second floor and walked down the corridor to its end. Oldham opened his door and we stepped inside.

He was living well. He occupied a two-room corner suite.

He closed the sitting room door behind us. "All right, Calhoun. What's on your mind?"

"Bribe money."

He crossed the room and sat down. "Who am I buying?"

"I don't know yet. You'll have to help on that angle."

He motioned me to a chair. "You're not making yourself exactly clear."

"I'll start at the beginning," I said, sitting on the edge of the chair. "It's simple enough. Hustin was murdered between nine and eleven at night. If we can offer evidence that she was here at the hotel, in her room, at that time, she'll be in the clear."

"It sounds too simple, too good to be true."

"The simpler the better," I said. "She really was in her room, but alone. We need a man to swear he was in her room with her."

"Why a man?"

"It'll look better to suspicious minds. If a girl had dropped in to visit—one of the hotel staff—the girl would have come forward by now. A man wouldn't have. Not until he saw she was in real trouble, worse trouble than having a man in her room."

Clarence leaned back, not taking his eyes from my face. "You couldn't be the man?"

"Kirk would never believe it, not if I told him at this late date. The same goes for you. It has to be someone else, someone whose thought of scandal has kept him silent so far. A chef, a waiter, a bellhop. The right man ought to be among the hotel help."

"By the right man you mean a man who can be bribed."

"You've been here awhile," I said. "You've observed them. It's my guess you miss little, if just through idle curiosity and speculation. You'd have noticed any man who might have paid attention to her."

Clarence smiled thinly. "Every hotel worker wearing pants has paid attention to her."

I settled back in the chair. I'd outlined it to Oldham. Now it was up to him. He would spot the man. He had the money. He pushed himself from his chair, walked to the window, and looked at Big Hominy. I wondered if he felt a little like a god, looking at the tiny town in the distance.

He turned again toward me. "You're slightly amazing, Calhoun. Too bad you were born out of place, out of time. However, you still haven't considered one point."

"Deaf Joyner?"

His brows jerked up. "Well! So you anticipate me."

"You leave Deaf to me."

Clarence looked at me a moment longer. Then he ended the talk by the simple expedient of crossing the room and opening the door.

"Come back about three o'clock, if that will give you ample time to see Joyner."

"Time enough."

He nodded, and I stepped into the hall, and he closed the door. He had made no promises, but I knew his end would be taken care of. He would find the man.

It took me a half-hour to drive out to Wolfhead Lake. The approaches gave visible evidence of Deaf's kind of care. The wooden fence at the private lake road was rotted away. The road was washed out in spots and the undergrowth on either side had grown unchecked. A grassy glade had been chosen for a dumping ground; it was littered with broken bottles, empty cans, and refuse that attracted flies.

Erected at random among the trees on the lake shore were several unpainted clapboard cabins. Deaf's house, weathered and leaning on its poplar-post foundation, stood on the hillside where the road stopped. The front yard was a clutter of cordwood, old ropes and chains, and rusty tools. A Model-A sedan with one headlight, three fenders, and no windows drooped beside the house.

Lula Mae, Deaf's common-law wife, was painting a flat-

71

bottom boat set up on a pair of sawhorses beneath a tall pine tree. She was wearing clothes of Deaf's—brogans, overalls, blue shirt. When she saw the car and who was getting out, she set down her paint can and brush and ran toward the house.

"Deaf! Deaf! It's Wade Calhoun. He's here! I warned you he'd come boiling out this way."

I followed her toward the house, walking natural and easy. I had just started up the plank steps to the sagging porch when Deaf appeared in the doorway.

He was a tall bony man, wearing only a pair of faded blue jeans held up around his thin middle with a piece of old sash cord. His features were gaunt. His hair was a mouse-colored mat grown long about his neck and ears. Some mountain wit years ago had tagged him with his nickname because of his hearing, more acute than a Cherokee's. The name had stuck.

When he appeared in the doorway, I stopped moving. His eyes were narrowed, and he held a rifle loosely in both hands. When a man holds a gun with such easy familiarity, it's more than a weapon. It's a friend; sometimes the only friend such a man has.

I kept my face composed, my eyes steadily on his. Then I moved to the porch.

"What you wanting here, Wade?" He tried to make it sound tough, but I had won the first little round.

"For one thing, I want to know if you're pointing that gun at me."

"I ain't pointing it particular. I just ain't wanting trouble."

"That's a hell of a way to keep from finding it. I don't

want trouble, either. But I don't like to talk to a man who's holding a gun on me."

"What kind of talk, Wade?"

"Friendly."

His gaze darted back to my face, seeking assurance. "You ain't armed, Wade?"

"Why should I be?"

"On account of you're sore at me for telling Kirk Hyder who I seen come out of the cabin the other night."

"Let Lula Mae frisk me."

She was standing close behind Deaf. He moved to one side to allow her passage through the doorway. She giggled as she slipped past him and patted my pockets and the waistband of my trousers.

"He ain't carrying arms, Deaf."

Joyner's bony shoulders relaxed. He smiled suddenly. "By hell, we've always been friends, Wade."

"Sure."

He reached the gun behind him, and propped it against the wall close to the doorjamb. "Lula Mae, bring me the fruit jar. Not the one with the white stuff in it."

Lula Mae scurried into the house.

"Sit down, Wade," Deaf said, motioning to a nail keg.

I sat down. He sat on the floor of the porch, near the door.

He draped his bony arms over his upthrust knees. "Nice day."

"Sure is."

Lula Mae returned with a fruit jar of amber liquor. Corn. But corn that had been buried in a charred keg until all the poison was gone. Joyner handed me the jar. I drank and passed it back. He drank as if the liquid were water.

"Mighty damn smooth stuff," he said, wiping water from his eyes with the back of his hand. "You can have a little one, Lula Mae."

Lula Mae drank about four ounces and set the jar beside Deaf. Then she moved to one side and filled her lower lip with snuff.

Deaf looked around at her. "Git on back to that boat."

"But, Deaf, I been working—"

"You heard me!"

She shuffled from the porch. Deaf watched until she resumed work on the boat.

"I'm glad you didn't come out here spitting blood and vinegar, Wade."

"I just wanted to talk with you about the killing."

"I'm always inclined to sociable talk, Wade. You know that. I told Kirk Hyder what I had to."

"Sure, Deaf. I'm not holding it against you."

"I'm mighty proud you're not gunning for me, Wade. Live and let live, I say." His gaze shifted over the unkempt yard, touched my face, moved to the lake.

"What was Rock running from, Deaf?"

"Trouble. I don't know what kind. He was pretty close-mouthed with me."

"How long was he here?"

"At my cabin? About four or five days."

"Did he have much company?"

"Not much. His brother came to see him couple or three days before the killing."

"Which brother?"

"Giles. The big mean one. The one that used to side Rock in mischief around here and in Tennessee. Rock sent word to Giles where he was staying. Giles slipped in one night. I taken a jar of corn over to Rock. Giles showed up and they run me off."

Deaf passed the jar over again. I had to drink or insult Deaf. I wondered if I were drinking from the side of the jar Lula Mae had used.

After Deaf drank, over a pint of whisky was gone from the jar. He set it down uncapped.

"Giles or anyone else been back to the cabin, Deaf?"

"Not that I know of. Kirk Hyder padlocked the cabin and put a notice on the door. I ain't supposed to rent it until he says it's okay. Nobody wanting it. Nothing unusual in there except a few bloodstains. 'Course there's a loose plank in the floor if you wanted to give the cabin a look." He gave me a grin, and I nodded satisfaction with his co-operative attitude.

"I'm more interested in what happened the other night than I am in the cabin, Deaf."

"I swear," he said, his face long with sadness, "I do wish I hadn't seen her, Wade. But I did. She cut right across that glade over there, and the moon was full on her face."

"Rock had no other visitors that night?"

"I didn't see 'em, if he did."

"He had one, earlier."

"If you say so, Wade." He had another drink. He didn't offer me one this time. He was beginning to feel nervous.

"Maybe somebody came earlier," he said. "I wouldn't say. I was bass-plugging the rushes over there in Jimson's Cove. You know, like an old hoot owl. Sleep all day, get restless at night."

"Why wouldn't you say, Deaf?"

"Well, now, Wade, I—"

"What time did you see her?"

"Don't recollect exactly."

"It was after midnight, wasn't it?"

We sat without speaking for several moments. He turned his head slowly, looked at me, and then watched Lula Mae paint the boat. "It could have been after midnight, Wade," A hardness came to his gaunt features. "I'm not saying it was. I didn't have no reason to notice the time."

"I can give you a hundred reasons."

He unclasped his arms from about his knees and leaned against the porch wall. "You sure you got 'em to give?"

"I wouldn't promise if I couldn't deliver."

"When would that be?"

"When Kirk Hyder decides she went into the cabin and came out after midnight."

"You're sure set on that time."

"Rock was killed no later than eleven o'clock. She wouldn't have stayed in there with a dead man for over an hour. Even Kirk wouldn't claim that."

Deaf ran his hand through his hair. "I ought to think about this some."

"There isn't time."

"I'd hate to tangle with Kirk . . ."

"You're running no risk at all, Deaf. You'll be backing up what is true. You've got to believe she didn't go to the cabin until after midnight."

Deaf picked up his jar, had a drink, and reflected on the remaining whisky without speaking. I stood up, feeling empty with despair.

"It's up to you, Deaf. I don't really need you. You've got

me off the lake and home a time or two when I was in no condition to be fooling around in a boat. I thought I ought to throw a chance to make a hundred dollars your way."

"Aw, hell, Wade, you know I ain't had a hundred in one piece in better than a year." He pushed against the floor with his hands and gained his feet with the agility of a monkey. "You know, right after I seen Vicky come out of the cabin, I came in the house and Lula Mae woke up. She asked me what time it was, and I had to look at the clock. When Rock was found, and the law come busting around, I got so unsettled I forgot. Now that I've had time to simmer down, though, I remember. What time you reckon it was, Wade?"

I looked at him levelly.

He grinned. His lips and gums looked slimy wet. "Twelve-twenty," he said.

I nodded and went down the porch steps quickly. I wanted to get away from there fast, before Deaf had a chance to change his mind.

11

BACK AT the Stonewall Jackson, I went directly up to Oldham's suite. He answered my knock, not stepping aside immediately. "Joyner?" he asked in a low tone.

"Set. How about your angle?"

He made a small motion with his head toward the interior of the room. I stepped in, and Clarence closed the door.

A boy stood near the windows. He was a man in years—early twenties, I guessed—and a man in build, trim, husky, wide-shouldered. But I automatically thought of him as a boy. His face was boyishly handsome, without a blemish. His hair was blond, waving softly back from a high widow's peak. His eyes were baby-blue, wide and bland. About his mouth hovered an expression of spoiled petulance.

Oldham introduced us. The boy was Delbert Sykes, a waiter. He crossed the room to shake hands. His every movement was studied, as if he were extremely aware of his good looks and athletic build. His handshake was limp.

"Calhoun will tell you what's on his mind," Oldham said.

I glanced at Clarence. "You haven't told him?"

"I'm merely a go-between. You asked me to find someone who would do a slightly shady job. For the proper pay, of course. I've sounded Delbert out. I think he would serve the purpose you have in mind, Calhoun." Oldham's smile was thin.

"You don't believe in sticking your neck out, do you?" I said.

"I have nothing to do with it," Oldham said. "Delbert has consented to listen."

"With reservations," Delbert said.

Oldham glanced at him. For the first time I saw a real expression cross Oldham's face. Raw distaste. Delbert was looking at me and missed it.

"I've watched Delbert about his work and studied him," Oldham said. "The old ladies among the guests will bribe the headwaiter to be placed at Delbert's table. Wouldn't surprise me if Delbert marries luxury one of these days, luxury held in ancient, tottering hands."

Delbert was hard to insult. He remained bland. "One has to look out for one's self. Now what is this chore, Mr. Calhoun? Mr. Oldham assures me it will earn a nice bit of money and entail no real danger."

Oldham rubbed the back of his neck. As his hand came away, he was holding up three fingers. "I'm sure you'd like to discuss business in private."

With brisk steps Clarence went into the bedroom. He closed the door, and I stared at the walnut paneling. I wondered what sort of guaranty Oldham required before he left a single track uncovered. He wanted things arranged so that I alone would be in the middle should the alibi fail.

Well, damn him! I didn't need him. He was no friend. Somehow or other I'd rake up the money to do the paying off myself. Vicky wouldn't owe him a thing.

"You look quite angry, Mr. Calhoun," Delbert said. "Perhaps I should leave, if this entails—"

"It entails nothing but a simple statement," I said. "Sit down."

He sat down with cautious movements. He drew a gold

cigarette case, beautiful worked, from his inner coat pocket. I wondered which rich old biddy had given him that present. He offered me a cigarette, but I didn't take one.

He lighted one for himself, a king-size with an ivory tip. I glanced at his clothes. Camel's hair sport coat, expensive slacks. All on a waiter's pay.

My appraisel brought a cynical smile to his lips. "I get along, Mr. Calhoun. Incidentally, I'm waiting."

"You know Vicky Hustin?"

"But yes," he sighed. "Lovely, lovely."

I had the urge to slap the weak-mouthed, boyish face. I walked over to a chair and sat down.

"Mrs. Hustin's husband was killed three nights back. Between nine and eleven o'clock."

Delbert took a dainty puff from his cigarette and said nothing.

"Mrs. Hustin was in her room at the time of the killing," I said. "Have you ever been in her room?"

"Oh, I've dropped in for a chat now and then."

"You were friendly with her?"

"As friendly as she would permit, when I hadn't other obligations on my time."

"Did you have obligations three nights ago?"

"Mr. Oldham has already asked me that. I had none."

"None that you've mentioned so far," I said. I leaned forward, my elbows resting on the arms of the chair, my fingers clasped. "Today, however, the hotel was rife with gossip. She was in trouble and had been caught. You know nothing of the killing, but you do feel now that you should volunteer the information that you were in her room from about eight o'clock until about eleven-thirty."

He snuffed out his cigarette, found his hands useless, and lighted a second.

"Really, Mr. Calhoun, I don't feel I should involve myself with the police."

"You're not involving yourself in anything! You know nothing about Rock Hustin or what happened to him. She was in her room. You're only substantiating the truth."

He took out a silk handkerchief and wiped his palms. "Are you sure that it wouldn't be dangerous?"

"Think of it for yourself, Delbert. How could it possibly be dangerous? You went to her room after you were both through work. You visited awhile. Then you went to your own quarters. What harm can come to you from saying that?"

He licked his lips. He was weakening. It was written all over his face. A lie meant nothing to him as long as it couldn't hurt him. "It happens that I badly need five hundred dollars, Mr. Calhoun."

His kind always needed money. "All right, I won't quibble." I stood up. Without taking my gaze from Delbert, I called, "Clarence."

He came out of the bedroom.

"Can you lend me five hundred dollars?" I asked.

"I think so. I'll get it from the hotel safe downstairs."

Clarence went out. Delbert continued to sit. He was taut. He lighted a third cigarette.

I remained standing, looking at him. I had a moment of misgiving, of wondering if Oldham had been very wise in his choice of men. Then I reminded myself that Oldham would have chosen the best available. It was Delbert or no one. Delbert or no alibi. No alternatives. We had to depend on Delbert.

81

"Now I've got to brief Vicky—Mrs. Hustin," I said. "At the moment, the time element should be meaningless to you. So it must be Vicky who calls you to Sheriff Hyder's attention. When I leave the jail, she will tell Hyder that she's learned from me that Rock was killed between nine and eleven. She will say that she can account for that period of time. You were visiting in her room. Hyder will come up to see you or send for you. All you have to do is say that you were there. Have you got it?"

"I think so."

"You can't think! You have to know!"

He jumped. "I know, Mr. Calhoun."

"Okay. Now how did you spend the three and a half hours that you were together in her room?"

He looked up at me. Those wide, blank, pretty blue eyes almost made me despair.

Then he began speaking slowly. "I passed her door. It was open and the light was on. I stopped and said hello. We gabbed about the day's work. I asked her to go out. She said she was too tired, but suggested we could play some gin. We played awhile, became hungry, and I went to the kitchen to rustle some eats. Before we ate, I went to my room and got my record player—a very fine player, Mr. Calhoun, hi-fi. We ate and listened to records. I left her room about eleven-thirty. I noticed the time when I went back to my room and set the alarm clock."

For a second, I stared at him. I relaxed somewhat.

"It sound okay?" he asked.

"Fine."

He looked pleased.

"What records did you listen to, Delbert?"

"Oh, some Glen Miller reprints," he said without hesitation. "*Chattanooga Choo-Choo, A String of Pearls* and some old T. Dorsey stuff. I'm a great admirer of the trombone, Mr. Calhoun." He snubbed out his cigarette. "It wouldn't be wise to pinpoint each title, do you think? To be too explicit might make it ring false."

Clarence came in and handed me an envelope. I passed it to Delbert. He opened it, flipped through the bills inside, and smiled up at me.

"Good day, Mr. Calhoun." He left the room quickly.

I glanced at Oldham. "You're afraid of him."

"I did the best I could." Oldham shrugged. "You can't make a silk purse out of a sow's ear, but you can make a small one of pigskin."

"I hope you're right." I turned toward the kneehole desk that stood against one wall of the room. "I want a pencil and some white paper."

"Help yourself."

I tore off the letterhead to give me a small sheet of white paper. I wrote in small letters with pencil:

Vicky, the alibi: You have just learned from me that Rock died between nine and eleven. You can account for that time. You were in your room with Delbert Sykes. You played gin, ate food he snitched from the kitchen, and listened to some Glenn Miller and T. Dorsey records. He left about eleven thirty. Repeat this, and nothing more. Everything is arranged. Destroy this note. Chew it up and throw bits of the pulp from the window, or swallow it if necessary. Chin up, darling. You'll soon be free.

I folded the note into a small square and slipped it into the pocket of my shirt.

Blank of face, but with his eyes brisk and frosty, Clarence stepped away from the desk. "You think of everything, Calhoun."

"I may not be able to talk to her privately, but I'll find a way of slipping her the note."

At the door, I paused. "You think of things youself, Clarence. You've carefully planned it so that if this thing blows up, I'll be in the middle."

"But I'll be free to work for her release. That's what you want, isn't it? Her release?"

"Of course it's what I want! I want something else, too. Since you're so anxious to stay clean, I want that five hundred regarded as a loan. I want to owe you absolutely nothing."

He put the tip of his forefinger against the bridge of his nose and adjusted his glasses. Then he smiled. "You know, Calhoun, the really interesting part is still to come. When she's free. When you lose her for good."

I slammed the door behind me, and I heard him laugh. I broke stride and stopped. I had to force myself to take a long, deep breath.

12

Josh Loudermilk was the only occupant of the sheriff's office when I went in. Kirk had been driving him hard, and Josh was catching up on his sleep, feet on his desk. He was blowing tiny spit bubbles as he snored.

I turned and started from the office. Then I heard him grunt. "Where you think you're going, Wade?"

"Up to see if Vicky needs anything."

He stood up and stretched, smacking the taste of sleep from his mouth. "Damn swivel chair's give me a crick in my back."

He frisked me, patting my clothes lightly. "I guess you're okay."

"No guns, files, or sticks of dynamite," I said.

Josh put his hands against his back and bent his crick far backward. Then he shuffled from the office. I followed him to the third floor. He opened the barred section door, which permitted us to talk with only her cell door between us. Josh lighted a cigarette and took up a stance beside the section door. I moved past him to her cell.

Hearing us, she had moved to the cell door. She reached between the bars to take my hand. Her face was shadowed with strain, and there was a question in her eyes.

"How are you, Vicky?" I had the note from my shirt pocket in my hand.

"Fine, Wade." Her fingers closed over the note.

We talked casually for a few minutes. Then I brought Rock's name into the conversation by mentioning that he was still at Daley's. I added the time of the killing, as Daley had given it to me.

"If you're going to start talking about the case," Josh called back, "let's break it off. I need a cup of coffee anyway."

I told Vicky I would see her later and rejoined Josh. We rode the precarious elevator down together.

Kirk was back in his office. He was seated at his desk, but as we passed in the corridor he came quickly to his office door.

"Wade."

I stopped and turned. Josh stopped also; then walked toward Kirk. "You need me?"

"No, I just wanted to ask Wade how his head feels today."

"The head's okay."

"How about the fingers? Clean?"

"As a fresh-bathed baby's."

"That's fine, Wade," Kirk said. "I thought that two trips to the Stonewall Jackson today might mean you were up to something."

His unfathomable blue eyes gave me the feeling he could penetrate every expression on my face. I wondered if he'd seen just how much of a jolt his words had given me.

"You've no right to shadow me, Kirk!" I said angrily.

"You should welcome it, Wade. If you're clean, it'll put me on your side. In case anything should happen, you couldn't have a better witness than the sheriff himself."

His face was as stern as a frosty granite peak. He was positive of his rightness, beset by none of the fears and misgivings common to most men. His confidence was great enough to shatter anything smaller that got in its way.

"Remember what I've said, Wade." He went back in his office as if the matter had been settled for good.

The office doorway swam in my vision. I felt Josh's hand on my arm. "Take it easy, Wade, take it easy!"

My fists uncurled into hands and some of the trembling left my arms and legs. I went outside with Josh.

As we crossed the square, he said, "How about that coffee?"

"No, thanks."

He watched me turn toward the Old Homestead. Then he went on to the café.

I walked the floor of the tired old room, trying to rebuild a confidence that had caved in like a paper bag. I tried to visualize the alibi as Kirk would see it. His every suspicious instinct would be aroused. He would attack the alibi from every conceivable angle. But he would run into a simplicity of statement affording no chinks for him to drive a wedge into.

It would work. It must work.

I repeated the words aloud; they didn't sound very confident.

How about the note? Did it make things clear enough to Vicky? Would Deaf Joyner get drunk and make a wrong statement? Was Delbert too much of a coward to carry it off against an implacable old mountain man who had worn a sheriff's star forever?

I could have asked myself those endless questions until my nerve snapped. I recognized the anxiety and fretting as useless waste. I forced myself to a measure of calmness.

The room was my enemy, its silence filled with the questions, its closeness choking me. I walked quietly from the

room, left the hotel, and went across the street to the Home
Cooking.

The blue-plate special was corned beef and cabbage. The
food was tasteless, but I ate it anyway. Then I bought three
magazines and an Ashville paper in the drugstore and went
back to my room. I drew a chair over to the window. I tried
to read. The sight of the courthouse was too impelling. Finally, I quit trying to read, turned off the light, and sat at
the window in darkness.

I saw Josh come out of the courthouse, get in his coupe,
and drive away. Minutes dragged by without anything else
visibly happening at the courthouse.

Josh's coupe returned, entering the square at a fast clip.
He braked hard before the courthouse. The coupe stopped
with a jolt.

Josh got out, slammed the door, and hitched his pants.
Then the door on the other side opened and closed, expelling
a passenger. The light from a nearby street lamp touched a
carefully groomed blond head and outlined a wide-shouldered
physique. Delbert had arrived.

Together, Josh and Delbert entered the courthouse, Josh
opening one of the heavy front doors and motioning Delbert
ahead.

I sat hunched in the chair elbows on knees, wiping my
face now and then with a handkerchief. My eyes ached.

Traffic thinned and then ceased on the square. The side-
walks were empty. A pale moon threw shadows over the
silent streets.

Josh came out of the courthouse and drove off, alone. The
courthouse clock, ages later, struck eleven. At eleven-twenty

the courthouse lights went off. Several more minutes passed before a lone figure left the building.

He passed under a light on his way to his muddy sedan. Gaunt, raw-boned figure, iron-gray hair. Kirk.

The business day was ended at the courthouse. I looked at the dark building a moment longer. It held the fascination of a dungeon for me. The ache lanced from my eyes, along my temples, into my head. I wondered what had been said and done over there tonight.

I could only be sure of one thing. Delbert had gone in, but he hadn't come back out.

I stripped to my shorts, stretched out on the bed, and tried to go to sleep. I heard the courthouse clock strike one; then two. I didn't hear it strike three. I was dreaming fitfully.

I was awakened next morning by an insistent knocking on the door.

"Okay. I'm coming."

I pulled on my bathrobe and opened the door. Josh Loudermilk was in the hall, removing portions of his breakfast from his teeth with his goose quill.

"Kirk wants to see you, Wade, right away."

"What's it about, Josh?"

"Kirk'll tell you."

"Is it anything serious?"

"Just get yourself dressed, Wade, and never mind the questions. Kirk'll tell you everything when we get over there."

Kirk was in his office, waiting for me. He was standing, facing the door, when I entered with Josh close behind me.

Kirk motioned to a chair. "Sit down, Wade."

I sat down. He half sat on the edge of his desk, arms

folded across his chest. He looked at me several seconds; then he shook his head helplessly. "I guess some men are naturally cut from fool's cloth."

"I don't follow that crack, Kirk."

"Now you listen to me, Wade. You know what I'm talking about, and I don't want any runaround. The quicker you level with me, the better it'll be for all parties concerned."

I tilted my chair against the wall, glanced past Kirk at Josh. "What's he been drinking for breakfast, Josh?"

Josh shrugged and said nothing.

"Come off it, Wade!" Kirk said. "You know what I'm talking about. You arranged it as neatly as a mountain woman putting together a quilt pattern. But it's blown up in your face."

I was sick inside. With a detached feeling, as though I were watching a scene through glasses that threw images out of focus, I saw Kirk nod at Josh and heard him tell Josh to bring the Sykes boy in.

Josh went out. Kirk continued to lean against his desk with his arms folded. "You're in it up to your neck this time, boy. You came so close to causing a miscarriage of justice that I ought to slap you with every charge in the book."

Josh came through the office door, prodding Delbert Sykes ahead of him.

Delbert showed the results of a night in jail. His hair was limp, falling about his pale face. His shirt was wrinkled. He needed a shave.

He saw me, looked as if he wanted to bolt from the office, and jerked his gaze away. I knew he wouldn't look directly at me again.

"This the man, Mr. Sykes?" Kirk asked.

Delbert touched his lips with his tongue. "Yes," he said, almost inaudibly.

"Not a single doubt in your mind?"

"No, sir."

"All right," Kirk said. "You can go back to the hotel now. Stay there. I'll let you know if I need you again. And if you have any trouble, you let me know."

"Yes, sir." Delbert turned and walked quickly from the office.

Kirk sat down behind his desk. A vein was pulsing in his temple. "You almost did something nobody has ever done before, Wade. I've made mistakes. I've been shown I was wrong. A few times I've failed. These things a man can take in stride. There are some he can't. Being made a fool of is one of them."

We regarded each other for a moment in silence.

"You want to know what broke it for you, Wade?" he asked. "Delbert's record player. She told me the story last night. It sounded reasonable, even convincing. Josh brought Delbert Sykes down and the details of his statement agreed well enough with hers. I took the precaution of jailing him as a material witness. This morning I canvassed the hotel help. I wanted to know if anyone had seen him enter her room or had heard the record player. No one had heard it— because the salad girl had it.

"She'd borrowed the player a few times in the past. She was on her way to a party at a summer house on the lake. She'd been busy all day and had forgotten to ask Delbert if she could borrow the player. As soon as she was off work she stopped by his room. He wasn't in. She was certain he wouldn't mind her using the player, so she took it. She re-

91

turned it the next morning. The whole thing was of such little importance to her that she hadn't mentioned it—until she heard a few of my questions.

"Delbert was about as tough as stale ice cream on a hot day, after that. He cried like a child. He said you threatened him with desperate bodily harm unless he backed up Vicky's statement. None of it was his fault. You forced him."

"You believe that, Kirk?" I said through stiff lips. "Isn't it more plausible that I bought him?"

Kirk shrugged. "I've repeated the gist of his statement. I don't care anything about Delbert, or even about you. One thing at a time, I say. The woman upstairs is the project right now."

He leaned back in his swivel chair. "Anything you want to say, Wade?"

"No."

He glanced at Josh, and Josh shuffled over to me.

"Let's go," Josh said.

We started out.

"Wade," Kirk said in a way that caused me to stop and turn and look at him, "I'll give you something to sleep on tonight. Know what you've done? I'll draw you a picture. You're a juryman and the prosecutor brings out this attempt to fake an alibi. It would pretty well convince you she was not in her room at all, wouldn't it? I've got everything I need. She knows it. You know it." He clasped his hands on the desk in front of him, looked at his thumbs, and his face looked tired for a moment. "I think the most merciful thing I can do is bring her to trial as quick as I can. Once it's over, maybe even you'll simmer down."

Josh took me upstairs and locked me up. The clang of the cell door was like a jolting, physical blow.

Josh thumbed his hat back. "Got any small needs, Wade? Cigarettes, candy?"

"No."

Josh studied me as if trying to fathom what went on behind the mask of my face. "It beats the hell out of me," he said with a shake of his head. "You could've had your pick of the daughters of the best families in town. A papa-in-law to give you a business loan. Using your head, you could've settled in a nice safe berth. As it is, what have you got?"

"Am I supposed to thank you for the advice?"

"The hell with it," Josh said, rebuffed. "It's your neck."

He stalked off. I watched him until he turned the ell into the corridor.

I had been in jail no more than a half-hour when Josh brought two visitors to my cell. They were Evalina and Mrs. McCall.

Evalina's face showed how hard it was for her to see a son behind bars. Vicky's mother trailed behind like a faded gray shadow, head bowed, hands gripping tight a patent-leather purse that was cracked with age. She wore gingham faded, patched, but neatly ironed. Her black, flat-heeled Mary Jane shoes had been rubbed with oil to help make her presentable as she trekked from Spivey Mountain to the town jail that held her daughter.

I offered the ladies my bunk and the wooden stool for seats. Evalina sat down on the edge of the bunk, her back erect. Mrs. McCall started toward the stool. Evalina looked at the bent, work-broken figure. She touched Mrs. McCall's

93

gnarled, calloused hand. With her other hand, she patted the bunk beside her. The gesture was friendly, and Mrs. McCall sat down beside her, embarrassed at being seated by a lady of quality.

Evalina looked at me. There was contrition in her eyes. She was assuring me she was sorry for the stand she'd taken against me, the thing she'd told Kirk that had led to Vicky's capture.

"Mrs. McCall was kind enough to call on me," Evalina said.

Mrs. McCall looked at the floor. "Hap came home with his head banged up from a piece of stovewood. I learned what you had tried to do for my daughter, Mr. Calhoun. I didn't know where to find you. I went to speak my obligation to your mother."

She raised her head slowly. "You're the kind of folks, Mr. Calhoun, that Vicky always wanted to be. Real quality. I —I went to your house today because I had to say my thanks, even if I got the door slammed in my face, knowing how a Calhoun's mother might feel about her son getting tangled with a McCall girl."

Evalina had decided on a course of action; now she followed it to the hilt. There was still the ghost of disappointment lurking in her face, but she brought a smile to her lips. "Our door will never be closed to you, Mrs. McCall."

"You treated me like a lady, ma'am. I'll never forget it."

Evalina glanced up at me. "Mrs. McCall and I braced ourselves with tea and talk, Wade. Two mothers consoling each other." She patted Mrs. McCall's hand. "I'm grateful and humble that I gained your confidence. Now you must trust Wade also, and tell him what you told me."

Mrs. McCall's shoulders seemed to grow narrower. "Ma'am, must I?"

"Yes," Evalina said softly. "I think Wade should know."

Mrs. McCall's chin rested on her bony, sunken chest. A soft, short sob came from her.

"He'll despise me," Mrs. McCall said.

"No, Wade will understand," Evalina insisted gently.

Mrs. McCall's voice was muffled, a whisper almost too soft for hearing. "She isn't his," she said.

I didn't understand for a few seconds. It was her humble, penitent manner that gave the pronouns meaning.

I was glad neither of them had taken the stool. I sat down on it. I understood now why Hap had hated Vicky, why he'd told me in the old Stillman cabin that she was no daughter of his. He'd meant it literally.

"Who is her father, Mrs. McCall?"

"A man you never knew, Mr. Calhoun. He's dead now." She was silent. For her, I suspected, the bars and brick walls had melted away. Then she said in the same low whisper, "Like Vicky, I hated the poorly mountain holler where I lived. I ran away and came to Big Hominy that summer. I worked for tourists.

"We were young, and he was a fine man. He was taking over the family business, and had brought his papa to the hills for a rest. His mother was with them, and a younger sister. They lived like folks should—happy, and loving each other, and kind.

"I worked for them, and him and me we fell in love. I lived all the life any person deserves that summer, Mr. Calhoun.

"After that particular night, he begged me to marry him. I

95

told him yes, but in the clear light of day I knowed I couldn't. It wouldn't be right. It wouldn't work. I didn't know how to dress or talk or act. I couldn't learn fast enough to ketch up to his world. I figured I druther have the memory of his love than to see it stung to the quick and turned to shame when his friends met me and laughed behind our backs.

"I ran off. I stayed with a family over in Little Hungry and worked out my keep. He hunted for me. He even found out where I'd come from and went there. But he didn't find me.

"I went back to the holler and give in to papa's wishes, and married Hap McCall. I reckon Hap suspected the truth right at first. I don't think he ever did believe she was a seven-month baby. Finally he whipped the truth out of me, but not the name of her father."

She paused to draw breath. The exhalation quivered. "Hap has always hated her, Mr. Calhoun. Now he is in his pleasure knowing that she suffers."

She closed her eyes and rocked slowly back and forth. "Hap knows more about the killin' than he's told. He knew Rock was back several days before Rock's death. Him and Rock drank some together. Rock come by the house five days ago to get a bottle of 'shine from Hap. Hap's had him a secret delight for nearly a week now. I can tell.

"Finding out what Hap knows is another thing again, Mr. Calhoun. If Kirk Hyder questioned him, Hap would just say that he had seen Rock, had a drink with Rock, and knew nothing. That's all Kirk would get. You'll have to get things out of him that Kirk can't, Mr. Calhoun."

"If Kirk can't—"

"You ain't bound the way the law is," she said. The dullness was gone from her words. They were soft, and distinct, like the pronouncement of a sentence. "You can use methods the law can't."

She turned her head slowly. Her gaze fastened on mine. "You're the only good that's ever come to her, Mr. Calhoun. I don't reckon it's right for her to be cheated out of it, no matter what happens to me, or Hap, or the law itself."

13

Josh brought my lunch an hour after Evalina and Mrs. McCall had left.

"Collard greens and sowbelly," Josh said, passing the tin plate into the cell. "This ain't the Waldorf."

I took the plate absently.

"You," he said, "look like you're doing some heavy thinking."

"I want to see Clarence Oldham. Phone him for me, will you?"

"Sure. Say, I got some news you might want to hear."

"Later. Right now leave me with the swine food and tell Oldham I want to see him right away."

Josh started away from the cell; then he turned back. "You really ought to hear this news, Wade. Rock Hustin's body was claimed this morning."

Halfway to the wooden stool with the food, I stopped.

"That interest you, Wade?"

"You know it does. Who was the claimant?"

"Giles, that big mean brother of Rock's. The one Rock always trusted and chased around with." Josh rolled his eyes. "Remember the way the two of them could stop a conversation in a beer joint just by walking in? Rock could find his way around in the city and make the tough boys know he was there. But around here in his own bailiwick, Giles made Rock look like a sissy."

Josh permitted himself a shudder. "Giles was drinking a little this morning. Not arresting drunk. He went to Daley's funeral home, claimed the body, and came over to the square. Said it was a good thing she's locked up. Said husband-killers didn't last long where he came from. Said if she wasn't locked up, she'd have an accident before she crossed the square."

A breath of heat touched the back of my neck. "Kirk know about this?"

"Sure. Kirk went out in the square and talked to Giles. Warned him."

"That should give Giles a laugh. Kirk should have arrested him."

"On what charge?"

"It was easy as hell to charge me!"

"Yeah, boy, but Giles only made a little loose talk. You acted." Josh hitched his pants. "I'll tell Oldham you want to see him."

When Oldham arrived, I was standing by the window of the cell. The food was still in the tin plate, untouched. Oldham was not admitted to the cell. We had to talk through the bars.

"Your choice of men wasn't very good, Clarence. Delbert caved in."

"So I heard." Except for its aura of brisk attention, his lean face showed nothing.

"You were lucky," I said, "or you might be a cell neighbor. Delbert wanted to keep the money. He didn't mention it. Not mentioning it, he didn't mention you."

"What money, Calhoun?"

He met my gaze with a thin smile. He seemed perfectly calm, controlled. He made me feel that his mind was a shockproof piece of machinery, never faltering.

"So you gave Delbert no money," I said.

"No, I didn't. As I recall, you asked to borrow five hundred dollars. I lent it to you. It was your money that you gave Delbert."

I shook my head in disgust. "Okay, have it your way. But you're still not shiny clean enough to satisfy Kirk Hyder, if he knew the whole story."

"Nor dirty enough to be in serious trouble, Calhoun," he said coldly. "You might cause me some minor annoyance, but not enough to scare me."

He took off his glasses and wiped them with his handkerchief. "You're going about this all wrong. I told you it wouldn't be advantageous for you to be immobilized as long as she is in here. Why don't you simply ask me for help?"

His tone caused me to feel a flare of temper. I controlled it. Temper was, right now, too rich a luxury.

"Okay," I said, "help me."

He put his glasses on. "That's better. To what extent?"

"I want you to see a bail bondsman."

"Hyder has you charged with conspiracy. Bond has been set at three thousand dollars. A professional bondsman will charge ten percent of the total, three hundred. That's what you want?"

"Yes."

"I'll do it."

"Thanks, Oldham."

"It isn't for you," he reminded me.

Less than an hour's time showed Clarence to be as good as his word. Josh rattled a key in the lock and opened the cell door.

"Well," Josh said, "you're out again. I'd walk easy this

time if I was you. Kirk'll throw the key away if we bring you in again."

I waited until Josh closed the door. We walked down the corridor together.

"I want to see her, Josh."

He made no comment. We walked past the elevator, and Josh unlocked the door to the women's section.

Vicky stood as she saw me outside of her cell. She brought a smile to life, and it was just for me.

"Hello, Vicky."

"Hello, Wade."

"We tried."

"Yes."

"It almost went off. It will next time."

She reached between the bars and touched my face. "Whether or not there's a next time, thanks, Wade. You said you'd go all the way for me, and you did. Somehow I'm not so scared any longer. I don't feel so alone."

"It's because I love you, Vicky."

"When you used to say that, I thought you were just talking. A man on the make using flattery."

"I want to make you for keeps," I said.

"Wade . . ."

I reached both hands between the bars, pulled her up close. Two bars formed a narrow frame for her face. I bent my head and kissed her.

Behind me, Josh cleared his throat. "This ain't no lover's lane. Let's go, Wade."

I went downstairs with Josh and got my personal belongings from the sheriff's office safe. Kirk was doing paper work at his desk, busying himself to keep from speaking to me.

101

Anger and frustration were reflected in Kirk's jerky motions as Josh went about the business of checking me out.

As I put wallet and change in my pocket, Kirk threw his pencil down. "I hope you've had time to cool off, Wade."

I didn't say anything as I got my watch strapped on my wrist.

I didn't intend it, but my silence caused Kirk to jump to his feet. He slapped the desk. "Dammit, go home and stay there. If you get your head broken, part of the headache will be mine. The headache of running them down, bringing them in."

"Who, Kirk? Who wants to break my head?"

"Hap McCall hankers to catch you on the business end of a stock of stovewood, and Giles Hustin hasn't taken kindly to your efforts to free the McCall girl."

My hands were shaking a little. I forced myself to speak quietly. "If you don't want trouble in your county, Kirk, tell Hap and Giles. They're the ones hunting trouble, not me. But I'll defend myself—and if I find out who went to Rock's cabin that night before she got there, you're going to listen. The whole damn county is going to listen!"

I walked out of the office before he had a chance to say anything more. I'd already said the wrong thing, too much of it. But I felt better.

I reclaimed my jalopy from the courthouse parking lot where Josh had put it. I drove around the square, conscious of a few stares that came my way. I drove out to the house.

There was no one home. I supposed that Evalina was still in town with Mrs. McCall.

I ate a cold lunch of leftovers in the kitchen. Next I bathed and changed into fresh clothes. I kept thinking of Giles and

Hap. I wasn't consciously afraid, but there was a small, cold lump in the pit of my stomach.

Dressed in clean slacks and a long-sleeved sport shirt, I left the servants quarters where Evalina and I lived and went into the main part of the house.

I went directly to a room that had once been a den. Like shrouds, protective muslin dusters covered most of the furniture. Against the far wall was a gun case containing weapons that dated back to Revolutionary times. From muzzle-loading musket to modern carbine, the guns had one thing in common. Each had been primed and fired by Calhoun hands.

I lifted a revolver of 1918 vintage from the case. An officer's sidearm, my father had carried it through the Argonne.

I unbuttoned two buttons on my shirt, and slid the gun into the waistband of my pants, next to the skin. With my shirt buttoned again, it hardly showed.

14

TWILIGHT WAS darkening the perpetual purple haze over the Smokies when I drove out to Deaf Joyner's fish camp. I stopped the jalopy in Deaf's cluttered yard and got out. Had it not been for the thin curl of smoke coming from the tottering chimney, Deaf's house would have looked deserted.

Then I saw Lula Mae at the corner of the house. She had been to the springhouse up on the hillside. She was carrying a half-gallon jar of cold milk.

She stood at the corner of the house for a few seconds. When I moved toward the house, she darted around the corner.

I heard her soft, nasal cry: "Deaf, Deaf! It's Wade Calhoun."

I recognized urgency in her voice. I vaulted up on the porch, crossed the front room, and reached the kitchen just as Deaf came in.

He stopped moving so quickly he was balanced on his toes for a moment. Anger and fright showed in his long bony face. The expression vanished, leaving him wary.

Lula Mae had crowded behind him. She was in a crouch, glancing around his elbow.

"Well, it is Wade, at that, Lula Mae. I heard your alibi scheme blowed up, Wade. I don't get my hundred dollars, huh?"

"Did you earn it?"

"Your plan didn't hold together long enough for Kirk Hyder to get around to me. I never had no chance to tell him it was after twelve when I saw her. I reckon, though, I ought to have a little something. I was willing to go through with it."

"All right, Deaf. I won't forget. I'll make it worth your while. I'll see that you get the whole hundred—if you tell me where Hap McCall is."

He came into the kitchen with a loose-limbed stride. Lula Mae slipped in and set the milk on the table, next to a plate of greasy pork. She opened the kitchen safe, a small wooden cupboard with doors covered with screen wire, and set out a bowl of peaches steeped in sugar and a jar of tomato pickles.

"Set and eat," Deaf said, "and we'll talk."

I pulled up a cane-bottom chair and sat down. Deaf would have interpreted a refusal in a personal way.

Deaf sat across the table. He slapped Lula Mae's behind sharply with the back of his hand. "Get out another plate and pour Wade a cup of coffee.

Lula Mae reached across my shoulder to pour coffee from a blackened, stone-enamel coffeepot. I added milk and sugar to the bitter, chickory-flavored brew. "How long was Hap here, Deaf?"

"We can talk business when we're done eatin'," Deaf suggested. He filled his plate and fell to in a way that reminded me of a shaggy wolf going after food.

I looked from Deaf to Lula Mae. Her gaze dropped quickly. I kept watching her. She turned toward the stove. Her growing nervousness almost caused her to drop a kettle.

Deaf loaded a tablespoon with food. When it was half raised to his mouth, I reached across the table and caught his wrist. "Hap's still here, isn't he?"

"Now what makes you think he was here at all, Wade?"

"I spent the afternoon asking around town. I kept missing him. He was last seen headed this way."

"Ain't no sign he stopped here."

"No sign he didn't, either. He'd been drinking, was drying out, and needed a jug."

From the lake came a popping sound as someone tried to start an outboard motor. Deaf's fingers went lax on the spoon. The spoon clattered on the table, scattering its greasy load of food.

I shoved Deaf's hand away and bounced to my feet. My chair fell backward with a clatter.

I started toward the door. Deaf rounded the table, heading me off. He entreated me with his hands. "Wade, there's been one killing out here. I swear I can't afford any more trouble."

"I merely want to talk to Hap."

"He's feeling mean as a snake. He told us how you banged him up with a piece of stovewood. He'd as soon kill you as spit, Wade."

"Thanks for the interest, Deaf. Now got out of my way."

'He stayed in the doorway until I had almost reached him. Sullen-faced, he moved to one side. "It's your own damned funeral, then!"

Three times the outboard motor coughed and failed to catch. By that time I was across Deaf's yard, almost to the edge of the lake. The floating bait shanty hid Hap from me.

The outboard came to life. This time it didn't die. Its throaty song of power sent blasting echoes over the lake. The boat swung from behind the bait house. It was one of

MAN - KILLER

Deaf's best rentals, a twelve-foot plywood craft. Powered with a ten-horse kicker, the boat moved with spirit.

Hap McCall was crouched in the stern. He made an adjustment in the fuel mixture and flung a glance toward shore. He turned the boat toward the open lake and let the motor out all the way. In a few minutes he would be out of sight. Once lost in the maze of coves, he would be impossible to overtake.

I ran the soggy length of planking that together with rope lashings, connected the bait house to deep-driven stakes on shore.

The tin and slab house rocked under my weight. I ran down the side of the house to its far corner. A dozen boats were moored with frayed Manila ropes around the bait house. Most of them were heavy flat-bottoms made of cheap pine planking.

One boat alone had a power plant other than oars. This was Deaf's boat, a fourteen-footer of plywood. On its stern reared a twenty-five horsepower kicker.

The boat was moored differently than the others, with a length of chain and a padlock. I looked around and saw a gaff hook with a short handle. I picked it up, knelt on the edge of the bait house, and inserted the tip of the gaff in a link of chain. I heard Deaf give a yell. I glanced over my shoulder. He and Lula Mae were running across the yard.

I gave the gaff a hard twist; a grating noise came from the rusty chain, but it held.

Deaf was yelling at me to stop. I threw another look toward him. He said something to Lula Mae. She stopped and ran back toward the house. I knew that Deaf had told her to get his gun.

MAN-KILLER

My palms were slippery on the gaff handle. My forearm muscles bunched as I put pressure on the chain. When the link snapped, I almost pitched from the bait house. I recovered my balance, tore the chain loose, and leaped across the narrow strip of water to the boat. I scrambled toward the stern of the boat, picked up an oar, and shoved off.

Deaf reached the bait house and ran out to its deep water side as I poled the boat too far away for him to jump. He spent a few seconds cursing and shaking his fist at me.

"Calm down," I pleaded. "I'm just borrowing it. I've used it before."

"Damn you, Wade, if anything happens to that boat—"

The roar of the motor as it started cut off anything else Deaf might have said. I leaned down the mixture, threw the kicker into forward gear, and opened it up.

I gave the lake ahead my full attention. I was hitting the ripples of Hap's wake; they were hard as stones with the big kicker driving the boat into them. I saw Hap swing around a point of land ahead.

I followed, gaining on Hap with every turn of the prop. Beyond the point, the lake spread over what had been a small valley years ago, before the building of the large power dam. Offshoots of the lake were visible as the water followed the contour of the hills. Dead ahead the land rose in two steep promontories which formed a narrow channel.

Hap kept the throttle to the last notch as he pointed the boat toward the channel. I pulled closer to him and we flashed between the twin promontories. Beyond the channel the lake widened again, a quarter-mile across, hills on all sides.

In the middle of the expanse of placid water, I saw the

suspicious swell. A water-sodden log was floating just under the surface. Hap failed to see it.

He struck the log at full speed, a glancing blow. The far end of the water-logged sapling shot out of the water. The near end, slippery and with the resilience of the water beneath it, failed to crush the keel. The boat flipped to one side, taking a wash over the freeboard. Hap was catapulted from his seat. He struck the water with a smashing impact that showered spray for twenty yards. The pitching boat righted itself and ran down the lake like an animate, frightened thing. I knew the empty craft would beach itself somewhere on the far shore.

I pulled the throttle down to slow position and circled the spot where Hap had gone under. He bobbed to the surface, gagging and trying to scream for help. I leaned far over the side of the boat, caught the collar of his denim jacket in my fingers, and pulled him toward the boat.

Incoherent whimpers were coming from him. He tried to fight his way over the side of the boat in his panic. His thrashing weight almost capsized the craft.

I hit him across the side of the face with the palm of my free hand. Some of the hysteria left him. He was able to utter a few limp curses at me as I dragged him the rest of the way into the boat. I gathered from the curses that I was a dirty dog who'd tried to drown a man who couldn't swim.

He lay across the boat like a collapsed gunny sack. He was violently ill for a few moments, vomiting over the side. A spasm of gagging coughs shook him. When this subsided, he lay spent and trembling.

At last he was able to sit up. Water dripped from his

jacket and overalls. Most of his face was pale, but the old scars on the left side of his face pulsed blood red.

After he'd sat up, Hap didn't make a move. I was standing over him, and the point of the gaff hook in my hand was touching Hap's throat.

15

HAP'S WRECKED face was a gargoyle mask. He inched away from the gaff, trying to smile.

"Lookee now, Wade, you wouldn't be taking a little drunk talk so serious? Any man might make some drunk threats if he'd had his noggin broke with a chunk of stovewood."

"The fight in the old Stillman cabin is a closed incident as far as I'm concerned," I said. "You had a knife. I had a club."

"Then what is it you're wanting?"

"Some talk about Rock Hustin. The things he did and said in the days previous to his death."

Hap was breathing easier, rapidly appearing stronger. A wildcat possessed no better recuperative powers.

"Now what in pea-picking hell makes you think I know anything about Rock?"

"You were his pal from a long time back, Hap. From the time you forced a helpless girl to stand beside him and repeat marriage vows."

"That don't mean when he came back—"

"When he came back you saw him, drank with him, furnished him with whisky on at least one occasion."

"Who told you that?"

"Never mind. I know it's true."

"The drinking of whisky with a man don't mean you know his business."

"Often it does. I think it would in this case. Rock liked to brag. Vicky had demeaned him by escaping him when she was old enough. Rock might well have wanted to build himself up in the eyes of his ex-father-in-law. With a few drinks under his belt, he would have boasted of where he'd been, what he'd been doing, how tough he was. I want to know, Hap. I want to know what brought him up here, what he was running from."

Hap's recovery was sufficient for fright to give way to craftiness. He couldn't control the sly expression that flitted across his face.

"Wade, I don't believe you got the particular kind of guts it takes to dig my eye out with that gaff hook."

In answer, I took a step toward him. The boat rocked gently. I took another step and the hook touched his cheek. Then his breathing stopped. With a sudden motion, he fell backward, holding up his hand in entreaty.

"Wait!" he said in a hoarse voice. He pressed back, looking at the hook as he caught his breath. "Maybe you would, at that."

"No one would ever know," I said. "Deaf and Lula Mae might suspect, but suspecting isn't proving. There are plenty of places out here to hide a body, Hap."

He crawled a few inches further along the bottom of the boat, away from the hook.

"I swear, Wade, Rock didn't tell me much. You got to believe that!" He wiped his mouth with the sleeve of his wet jacket.

"Walk close to the truth, Hap. I'll find out if you lie."

"Think I'm crazy? Ain't no time for lying now." With extreme caution, he pulled himself up on the forward seat of the boat.

"Where'd Rock go when he left Knoxville two years ago?"

"Two or three places, he said," Hap replied. "He pulled a

couple little deals, but didn't run into anything to suit him. He stayed on the move for a good while."

"He settled some place?"

"You might call it that."

"Where was he before he came back here?"

"Jacksonville, Florida. He was working for a gambler, a bookmaker named Lee Stamey."

"What happened down there to put Rock on the run?"

"A heist. Rock lifted some money that belonged to Lee Stamey."

"How much?"

"Fifty thousand dollars."

I caught my breath.

Hap said, "Rock thought he had him a slicked-down deal. Thought it was all fixed so it would look like somebody else had taken the money. Lee Stamey hadn't trusted him. He'd watched Rock closer than Rock had figured. Rock got a tip just in time that Stamey was wise."

"Stamey was operating illegally?"

"That's it. Stamey couldn't go to the law. The money was the payoff on a big illegal bet. Rock figured to disappear, sit tight for a while, and slip from here to another part of the country. He might have made it, too, if she hadn't gone to the cabin that night. I told him he was a fool for not forgetting her. He couldn't get it off his mind that she felt she was better'n him and wanted no part of him."

Hap became silent. He looked up at me, beginning to shiver in his wet clothes. "That's all, Wade. I swear to it!"

"You'd swear to anything. When did you see Rock last?"

"Lemme see—two days before his death, I think it was.

Look I'm done in and freezing in these clothes. Can't we get off the lake?"

I stood to one side. "Start the kicker."

He crawled past me, started the motor at the second pull of the cord, and turned the boat toward Deaf Joyner's dock. The hills were black silhouettes against the deepening blackness of the sky; the wind was chilling Hap to the marrow.

The sound of the motor had Deaf standing at the end of his floating bait house. He craned his neck forward, straining his eyes to penetrate the deep twilight. He was sullen and silent as he threw a line. I snubbed it in the metal fitting on the prow of the boat. Deaf tied the line to one of the metal rings at the edge of his shanty dock. Hap had the motor putting in neutral. He cut it as I leaped from the boat to the dock.

Deaf watched Hap follow me from the boat.

"Where's my other boat?" Deaf asked. "At the bottom, I reckon!"

"Beached in Jimson's Cove. You can pick it up tomorrow morning," I said. I opened my wallet. I was almost broke, with nothing left but two tens and a five. I handed Deaf one of the tens. "Enough for your trouble?"

His manner thawed. He thrust the money into his pocket. "You know how it is. Man sees his boat getting took that way, he kind of loses his temper. Wouldn't want it held against me."

I assured Deaf that we were still friends. Then I told Hap that I wanted him to drive back to town with me.

"I got nothing more to say, Wade," he said.

"I want you to say it to Hyder."

He deliberated with himself for a moment. Then he

shrugged. "I don't see as it means anything. I'll repeat what I told you."

We went up to the house, crossed the yard, and reached my car. "You drive, Hap," I said. "I wouldn't want you jumping out of the car and skinning yourself up."

Kirk Hyder's face remained impassive as he listened to Hap. We were in Kirk's office. He hadn't been there when Hap and I had arrived in town. I'd had Kirk's second deputy, a lean, grave young man, call him over.

I watched Kirk lean back in his chair when Hap had finished speaking. "I'll check into it," he said.

"It wants more than a mere checking into," I said angrily. "Isn't it possible that Lee Stamey followed Rock up here and killed Rock to get his fifty thousand back?"

"Possible. Not probable. You forget, Wade, that this is a small town. If a city hoodlum had been around inquiring after Rock, I'd have known it."

My face felt hot. My throat was tight. "Dammit, what does a man have to do to make you *see!* How about the money? How do you account for it?"

"Maybe Rock hid it. Maybe he banked it some place. Or maybe there was no money at all. Hap says Rock was drinking. The whole thing could be a tall yarn for self-glorification."

"Then you'll continue the one path of investigation?"

His brows moved upward. For a second his face was blank with amazement. "Continue? Wade, I'm finished with it! A grand jury was called and sworn in today. By tomorrow night I'll have an indictment. A court term opens within a week. In less than a month, her waiting will be over." He made a cutting gesture with his hand. "Now get out of here,

Wade, and don't come back! By the devil, don't come back!"
I walked from Kirk's office feeling more alone than I ever
had before.

16

THE DOORS of the grand jury room opened at three thirty that afternoon. The first step was taken. Vicky was indicted for first degree murder.

I was in the square when I heard. The news left me numb. I'd known such an indictment was possible, but I simply hadn't been able to conceive of its happening.

I caught bits of talk as I passed small groups of excited people. If Rock had gone to her that night, the indictment might have been much less severe. A plea of self-defense might have meant no indictment at all. Instead, she had gone to him, sought him out, it was said, with the full intention of removing him from her life for good, regardless of the measures necessary.

The numbness had faded by the time I entered the Old Homestead. I made it up to my room and stood in the middle of the floor shaking as if I had a fever.

From the window, I looked at the street square, and courthouse. I saw Giles Hustin going from one group of people to another. He was laughing and shaking hands. He was a big solid man who moved with an astonishing agility and grace. He was wearing dark blue slacks and a sport shirt that strained across his chest. From the shirt his massive neck rose, a short column that spread into a square, heavy-featured face. His coarse black hair glinted in the afternoon sun.

Giles looked toward my window. He saw me, and stood laughing. Several men noticed the byplay and shuffled near him, until there was a taciturn, lantern-jawed semicircle at Giles' back.

Standing spread-legged and solid, not taking his eyes from the window, he half raised his hands. His arms were like young tree trunks. He placed his fists one atop the other and made a motion as if wringing a neck.

I leaned close to the window and hoped he could read the words I was forming with my lips.

Giles looked about him; the men hovering behind him laughed obediently. Giles slapped two or three of them on the back. He was the center of a group that crossed the square and entered a beer parlor.

When Giles' arrogant progress passed from view, I moved away from the window. One favorable thing had happened. The shakes had stopped.

My mind was operating in a clear, cold, detached manner. Hatred, fear, frustration—these feelings were suddenly gone.

I didn't need to rationalize, make excuses to myself, or talk myself into it. A thing needed doing, and I knew I was going to do it. Without remorse, I knew it. I knew it as if my mind had been a long time in silent, steady preparation of the idea.

I needed money, time, and luck.

I went downstairs to the lobby and shut myself in a phone booth. I called the Stonewall Jackson. Ten minutes passed before I was talking to Delbert Sykes.

"Wade Calhoun, Delbert."

A short silence ensued. "I—uh—honest, Mr. Calhoun, I meant—"

"I don't care what you meant to do," I said. "I know what you didn't do."

"The sheriff," he said, "the old buzzard scared the pants off me. Please . . ."

"You didn't earn your money, Delbert."

"I tried . . ."

"I'll give you an A for effort. You weren't paid on that basis. You were paid to do a job. The job wasn't done. I bought an article in good faith. When the can was opened, the contents were rotten. Now I want a refund."

"Look, Mr. Calhoun," he said in a choked voice, "I spent most of the money."

"How much is left?"

"Two hundred."

"All right, put the two hundred in a plain white envelope and send it to me at the Old Homested hotel, in town." I added, "She was indicted for murder today, Delbert."

"Oh, cripes," he said. "I'll have to testify at the trial!"

Only there wouldn't be a trial.

"How'd I ever get mixed up in this thing!" he said, making a soft moan of the words.

"For five hundred dollars," I said. "You thought it was bargain day."

An hour later the money was delivered by a messenger boy who said he worked at the hotel. Standing in the open doorway of my room, I accepted the envelope. I gave the boy five dollars, and he thanked me with a flash of white teeth.

I closed the door, ripped the envelope open, and counted the money. It was all there. I stuffed the money in my wallet and left the hotel.

I drove out to the Bar-B-Cue and bought a fifth of whisky. On the way back, I pulled to the side of the road. No cars were in sight. I held the bottle out of the window and poured half of the whisky on the ground. Then I took a small drink and washed my mouth with the raw liquor so that I reeked with the smell of it.

When I reached the square, I let the car creep, driving with the excessive caution of a man who knows he is drunk.

I took a long time parking the jalopy in front of the court-house; when I got out, the car was at an awkward angle, the front wheels a good three feet from the curb. I entered the courthouse walking straight but with a suggestion of limber-ness in my legs.

Kirk and Josh were in Kirk's office. The door was open. I burped softly, wandered into the office, and sat down. Kirk and Josh exchanged a glance.

I sat staring at the floor, morose, hoping that I looked stupid with drink. "All over," I said, dull pain in my thick voice. "All done. All finished."

"You're drunk," Kirk said.

"'S the truth. Wade Calhoun's drunk." I stood, pawed at Kirk's hand. "Want to 'pologize, Kirk ol' man. Caused you a lotta trouble. Jus' doing your duty. Fine sheriff, fine man. Ain't he a fine man, Josh?"

"Yeah," Josh said.

"Dumb," I said. "Tha's me. All loused up. Dame says she didn't kill her little ol' husband. I stick my neck out. Plenty dames. Plenty fun. Kirk, I hand it to you. Good sheriff. Let's me and you have a drink just to show no hard feelings."

Kirk moved away from my pungent breath with uncom-fortable distaste. "No hard feelings—but I ought to lock you up.

"For what?" I stared at him owlishly; then grinned. "That

all you think about? Lockin' Wade Calhoun up? Don't wanna be locked up. Goin' home right now and sleep it off. Soon's I get my car . . ."

"You set foot in that crate and you'll wake up tomorrow morning in the clink," Kirk said. "You'll sleep it off, all right. Across the street in your hotel room." He gestured with his head and said in a low tone, "Take him across the street, Josh."

"That's right, Josh," I said. "Room beginnin' to rock. Need a bed."

"And stay in it," Kirk said. "The minute you're seen on the street, upstairs you go."

"Won't cause trouble," I said. "Done causin' trouble."

I draped my arm across Josh's shoulders for support and we started from the room.

At the doorway, I pulled free of him. "How about my car? Good little ol' car sittin' out there in the street."

"Josh'll park it behind the courthouse," Kirk said. "The keys'll be on the desk here. You can pick them up tomorrow morning."

"That's fine. Good old Kirk."

"Get him the hell out of here, Josh!"

Josh and I crossed the square. As we started up the stairs in the Old Homestead, I let my knees buckle.

"Last drink," I said weakly. "Kind of hittin' me."

"Yeah," Josh said. "It's always the last one does it."

I let him help me into the room. I groped for the bed, touched it, fell across it.

Josh stood looking at me a moment. I heard him give a disgusted grunt. Then he went out, and I listened to his footsteps fade down the hall.

I rolled over and stood up. Standing back in the room, I could see a portion of the street. My distance from the window kept me from being seen from down there.

Josh came out of the hotel. I watched him cross the square. Thrusting his head in the open window of my car, he saw the keys in the ignition. He got in the car and drove it around the far corner of the courthouse.

When the car was out of sight, an upsurge of feeling almost choked me. As a private citizen I wasn't permitted to park the car behind the courthouse. I'd had to do it by remote control.

And now it was done. The car was in the precise spot where it would be needed tonight.

I waited in the room an interminable length of time. Darkness came. A pale moon rose from its hiding place beyond the jagged rim of the mountains.

The seconds passed like the drip of water from a tiny hole in a great container. A freshening night breeze stirred through the dark room. In the square below, activity gradually ceased. There was a fresh flurry of movement when the final feature in the movie house was over. The movie-goers didn't remain abroad long. A stillness rustled back across the square.

I reached under my shirt and pulled out the revolver. For the second or third time since Josh had brought me to the room, I broke the gun and checked its load.

I slid the weapon under my belt and put on a lightweight jacket. I gave one final look to the square. It was lifeless. I took a deep breath, moved to the door, and opened it.

The hallway was empty. I traversed its length quickly,

stepped through the open window onto the fire escape. A few seconds later I was in the alley.

I reached the sidewalk and heard voices, a muffled burst of laughter. A man on the sidewalk shouted goodnight to a few people still inside the beer parlor. His heels made hollow sounds as he came toward the alley.

I stepped back in the alley and pressed myself against the wall of the building.

The man paused at the mouth of the alley, a big, brawny shadow. I saw him stiffen. He was staring at the white blob of my face in the infiltrating light.

"Calhoun!"

It was Giles Hustin.

I walked toward him. I had the gun in my hand with the butt against my palm and the barrel pointed upward. He didn't see it.

He moved up to me. I could see the glint of red in his eyes and smell soured alcohol on his breath. He spat. I bunched and quivered all over when the spittle made a soft slapping sound against the front of my jacket.

"I've been wanting to talk to you, Calhoun. My brother's killing wants payment."

I kept from thinking about his spit hitting my jacket. I had money, two hundred and ten dollars would buy a lot of distance, and there might be time. But running into Giles was the kind of luck I was having. I needed to stay calm and hedge my final bet with every bit of control I could muster.

"I'm sorry about your brother, Giles, and I don't have any argument with you."

His breathing was gusty. He was working himself into a liquor-inflamed rage.

"You started the argument when you hid her out there at the old Stillman cabin," he said. "You've been too damn smart. I think you need taking down a peg!"

His face was twisted with a sadistic lust. He reached for me, expecting me to step back. Instead I stepped forward and slapped him on the side of the head with the gun.

He staggered and cursed. Before he could lunge, I hit again. He went to his knees. The third blow put him flat on his face.

He was out cold as I rolled him into the shadows at the base of a building. I was listening for sounds that would mean someone had seen or heard. The stillness over the square was unbroken.

It seemed impossible to get breath into my lungs. I crossed the square quickly. Seconds later I was inside the courthouse.

Kirk's second deputy, Luther Milhorn, stood at the desk in the sheriff's office and poured coffee from a thermos bottle into a paper cup. His serious face reflected the deep, unconscious sense of responsibility he felt toward his job.

He glanced over his shoulder and saw me. He set the thermos down. "Kirk said you were in the hotel, Wade. He told me not to take any monkey business if I got a call about you."

With Giles Hustin in the alley, I didn't know how much time I might have now. None to waste. Without saying anything, I pulled the gun from the cover of my jacket and pointed it at Luther.

His face reddened. "You won't get away with this, Wade," he said quietly.

"All I can do is try. Pitch me those car keys on the desk."

When I had the jalopy keys in my pocket, I said, "Now

those at your belt. The upstairs keys."

He unhooked the bundle of keys and tossed them to me.

"You alone, Lute?"

He nodded.

"Then let's go," I said.

He walked ahead of me with an easy stride. But he couldn't control his shoulder muscles. They began bunching as we neared the elevator.

"Open it," I said.

The grill slid back with a squeak and rattle. Lute's back was to me. I hated to hit him, but I knew what a long chance I'd take, even with the gun, if I rode up with him in the confines of the cage.

When the pistol swung down, Lute fell forward into the elevator. I stepped across him and pulled him until his feet were out of the corridor.

I started the cage bumping upward. I ran my tongue around the inside of my mouth; the dryness remained. I couldn't have worked up enough saliva to spit if my life had depended on it.

She was sleepless, standing at the window of her cell and looking at the rolling, moon-bathed mountains. She wasn't standing with shoulders sagging in defeat. She stood straight, as if in complete defeat she had found a strange kind of strength to help her face the end.

Then she heard the key in the lock of the section door. She turned quickly. At her back now, silvery moonlight burnished the copper of her hair.

As I opened the door of her cell, she reached toward me with a groping gesture. "Wade! How did you—"

"I'll explain on the way. We haven't much time, but we don't need much. Just a little; then freedom."

She made a sound that was half laughing, half crying. With my arm around her, we started from the cell.

The open door stopped her. I felt a slight tremor pass over as she pulled herself together.

"Wade, I can't let you do this to yourself." She touched my chin, pulled my face toward hers. Her eyes looked very deep. "You said I could believe in you, Wade. You said you'd go all the way. I only half believed. Now I believe with all my heart. I'll never forget. And for that reason I can't let you do it."

"Save the talk! I'm acting through pure selfishness. With you gone, what is there here for me? Days without purpose, endless, empty nights."

"If we fail?"

"But we're not going to fail, Vicky! Within an hour we'll be in Asheville. Tomorrow night a bleached blonde will slip from her hotel room. A man will explain to a rooming-house landlady that he's been called away suddenly. He'll pay room and garage rent for two weeks in advance, saying his jalopy is so old he doesn't want to drive it on his trip. That'll keep them from tagging us through the car. At least three weeks will elapse before the landlady reports the car to the police. By that time, the man and blonde will have met in Atlanta, stood before a justice in a little town somewhere in south Georgia—and vanished."

"Wade, people don't just vanish."

"Don't kid yourself! Police files are full of them."

"You crazy Calhoun! Kiss me."

I kissed her. She held to me for a moment as if still un-

126

able to believe that the door was really open. Then we were running on our toes through the corridor. The back stairs.

We were outside the rear of the courthouse, and the air was cool and sweet. The jalopy was where Josh had left it.

The starter ground. The motor coughed. Then it started.

I had to swing around the square to head out of town. As I did so, the headlights swept the alley where I'd left Giles Hustin. He was no longer there.

17

THE mountain road rushed at us like a wide flat rope uncoiling. Touched with the silver of the moonlight, clouds hovered over the far-flung peaks. Beside me, Vicky rode with her head resting on the back of the seat to catch the cool night air pouring through the open windows of the car.

A glint of light reflected in the rear-view mirror. A few seconds later the reflection showed again, and remained. There was a car behind us.

My immediate urge was to step down on the accelerator. Instead, I continued at the same rate of speed. I didn't want everything to reach an ironic end because a highway patrolman had picked me up for speeding.

The headlights came on fast, resolving from a glare to twin beams. There was no telltale revolving red light over the windshield. He wasn't highway patrol.

He swung out into the left hand lane of the narrow road.

"Get down," I told Vicky.

She slid down in the seat, resting her head lightly against my right side.

I heard the powerful surge of a motor pulling abreast. I glanced at the car. It was a heavy gray sedan. It was driven by a man. As he turned his head to look toward me, I saw his face in the glow from the car's dashboard lights.

Giles Hustin!

I gave the jalopy every bit of gas I could. The first man to reach the curve up ahead would be in a position to keep the other from passing.

Giles was taken with the same intent. His gray sedan began to move ahead. I edged toward the center line. My left front fender touched his right rear. Metal grated briefly; sparks showered like miniature stars dying in the moment of birth.

The sedan lurched, causing Giles to fight the wheel. I gained a few feet. I watched the curve rush closer; with luck I would get to it first.

Giles decided he still had time. The sedan's motor gave out a high keening sound. The car began to move ahead of me. Giles was rigid over the wheel, braced and prepared if I should try bumping him again.

The jalopy had done its best. It wasn't enough. We went into the curve with Giles half a car length ahead.

"Hold tight," I told Vicky. "He's going to ride us into the shoulder!"

I slammed on the brakes. The sedan flashed toward the inside of the curve without meeting the resistance of the jalopy.

I saw him cut back. A rear wheel touched the loose gravel of the shoulder. The car lurched and skidded into the wooden guard-rail with a noise like an explosion. One light went out. The other beamed into yawning emptiness as the sedan seemed for a moment to be an animate creature trying to tear free of the earth.

The silhouette of the car hung against the moonlit sky; then it was gone, rolling end-over-end with the noise of an avalanche.

I rested my forehead against the wheel and gave myself the luxury of a shudder. Beside me, I could feel Vicky trembling. But she reached forward and wiped some of the sweat from my face with the soft pressure of her hand. Then she opened the car door and started to get out.

I reached and caught her arm. "Vicky . . ."

"We've got to go down and see about him, Wade. He may still be alive, bleeding to death."

"And if he is?"

"We'll have to take him back."

I knew she meant it. She looked small and beaten and her face was pale in the moonlight; but she wouldn't buy her freedom this way.

"I'll go," I said.

I got out of the car. From the place where the guard rail had been ruptured I looked down the almost-vertical mountainside. I saw the car and started down.

The sedan had cut a swath through brush and small saplings. I made my way down as fast as I dared. Twice my feet slipped and I had to grab for a tree to keep from tumbling.

The sedan lay on its top, wheels up in the air. It gave out the suffused odors of radiator water and oil on hot metal.

I crawled close to the car. I didn't see Giles. I struck a match. The front door beside the driver's seat had been ripped loose and hung crookedly on one hinge. Giles wan't in the car.

I found him about twenty feet above the car. He was lying on his back, one leg crumpled beneath him, his arms upflung so that his hands were about head high. His face was like a mass of red jelly. His clothing was dirty, bloody, and almost ripped from his body. You could tell just by looking at him that he was dead.

The torn condition of Giles' clothing revealed a section

of canvas belting he was wearing next to his skin. I loosened the buckle and pulled the belt free of him.

My hands were shaking and my stomach was tight with a burning sensation as I stood with the belt in my hands. It was about three inches wide, sewn in sections. Each section was an inch thick with money. There were thousand dollar bills in the section I opened. I was incapable of movement right away. Giles, the one person Rock Hustin had trusted!

My mind did a quick survey. Rock had stolen the money from one Lee Stamey in Jacksonville and run for the fortress of the hills. Rock then had entrusted the money to his brother, no doubt promising him a cut. Why? Because Rock was was afraid. By passing the money to Giles, Rock had not only hidden it, he had had enlisted Giles' aid as well.

Giles, then, had had a double reason for his own actions, for wishing Vicky to die. He believed her guilty—his willingness to risk his neck to bring her to his conception of justice proved he believed that. His second reason, the money, would have been less emotional but no less potent. With Vicky paying for Rock's death, the case would be closed. Sheriff Hyder, would have no cause to search for the money on the level of a murder investigation.

Fifty thousand dollars. Here in my hands. Not two hundred and ten dollars to take us only to the edge of the shadow of danger. Fifty thousand could mean Havana, South America. Investment in a business. A real start.

A feeling of wild freedom came over me. I pulled out my shirt, loosened my belt, and wrapped the moneybelt around my waist. Then I straightened my clothes, nestled the gun under my belt, and started up the long, steep hillside.

The climb was hard. I tore my fingernails and scraped my

131

knuckles on stone. As my straining muscles tired, the real factors of our situation returned. My elation died.

I crawled over the rim of the road and stood up. Vicky rushed across the road to me.

"He's dead," I said.

"Then we go on."

18

WE HIT the road block ten minutes later.

I saw the highway patrol car swing out of an intersection halfway down the grade. He stopped broadside on the state road we were traveling. The revolving light over the windshield winked red. The patrolman was out of the car, hand on his gun; he stood in a wary attitude, prepared to use his car for cover, as he motioned for us to stop.

Giles had raised an alarm before leaving Big Hominy, or Lute Milhorn had regained consciousness. The exact event was of no consequence. It was enough to know the hunt was on. There was no question in my mind as to the prey they were seeking.

Less than three hundred yards of steep roadway separated the jalopy and the patrol car. The distance was lessening rapidly. I had no time to think or plan. I knew only that to stop would mean the end. We had no choice, nothing to lose.

I shoved Vicky down in the seat as I closed in on the patrol car. The state cop was a motionless figure caught in the glare of the headlights. Then with a cool, deliberate motion he pulled his gun.

I felt the jalopy lurch as I swung to the shoulder. Gravel from the shoulder showered underneath the car. The uneven traction caused the rear end to start swinging in the beginning of a skid. The wheel tried to tear free of my hands.

I wrestled the jalopy to something resembling a straight course. The car rocked violently as it flashed past the patrol car.

The state cop fired three times. Two of his shots were wild. The third cried briefly on metal in the rear portion of the car. I heard myself begging Vicky to stay down, stay down.

He fired twice more at the rear end of the jalopy as we dropped into the intersection. I turned the wheel hard to the right. Screaming tires painted a wide swath of burned rubber across the asphalt. I twisted the wheel to the left. The jalopy settled to a steady run. For the moment, the highway was empty. The point of the intersection hid us from the patrolman.

The road dropped down the reaches of Spivey Mountain in a long series of tight curves. Guard rails on two curves blurred past us. Then I slammed on the brakes and slowed enough to enter an old logging road that crawled up the mountain. I cut the lights, shoved the jalopy in second gear, and drove up the rutted lane with brush slapping at the car and the rear wheels spinning. Around a bend in the logging road, I turned off the ignition. I was unable to release the wheel. I dropped my forehead on my knuckles.

I wanted to blame Giles for this. I needed someone to blame. I could only blame myself. I had used up the needed margin of time fondling a thick moneybelt and letting my imagination run riot. Otherwise, we would have missed rendezvous with the patrol car and at this moment would have been well on our way toward the federal highway leading to Asheville. The patrol hadn't time or equipment to cover all possible roads in the area. They'd needed more than luck. They'd needed what I had given them.

I raised my head. Vicky's face was close to mine. With a soft cry, she was in my arms. We held each other for several

134

minutes without saying anything. We were small, alone, and lost, and the night was an impersonal, alien thing.

"Listen," I said finally, did you ever have a strange feeling come to you, a certainty that something was going to happen?"

She looked up at me quietly.

"We're going to make it," I said. "I feel it. There's a force keeps pulling us together, taking us over the hurdles. Can you believe that?"

"Why not?" she said after a moment. "There's a force keeping the stars in place and bringing the oak out of the acorn." Her face came closer to mine. "I've needed you for a long time, Wade."

I kissed her then, wishing there was more time. I told myself there would be time, and released her.

I turned the ignition key and started the car. The motor fired, but ran only a short time. Despite my coaxing, the motor refused to run again.

I cut the ignition and glanced at Vicky. Her hand caught my arm. "I smell gasoline, Wade!"

I could smell it too.

I opened the door and got out. I traced the smell of gas to the rear of the car. The smell was very strong there.

I heard the final drops of gas falling from the tank onto dead leaves. The trooper's shooting had been more effective than I'd thought.

Vicky came around her side of the car. Her face grew pale. She sank to her knees and looked at the gasoline-soaked leaves glistening in the moonlight that filtered through the trees.

I tried to keep bitterness from my face. My high certainty

135

of a moment ago was only a memory. The last drop of that certainty splashed from the tank to the leaves.

Then the night was very silent.

She stood up and came toward me. "We can't quit now," she said.

"We won't quit," I said. "We'll give them plenty of trouble, make them seek us out, run us down. We'll stay here on the mountain, and we'll treasure every moment of freedom. . . ."

A bright, new sun pushed the shadows deep in the cave. I woke slowly; then I rolled over and sat up. Vicky wasn't in the cave.

I felt panic. I crawled to the mouth of the cave and pulled myself upright. Half the world was visible, endless rolling mountains and valleys. But no Vicky.

Then I saw her coming down a path twenty yards to the right of the cave. The morning breeze touched her hair and dress. She gave me a smile. "Have a good sleep?"

"Yes, but a bad waking. You were gone."

"I crossed the ridge," she said, "and spied on the house until I saw Hap leave. I brought something from my mother."

She was carrying a small wicker basket on one arm. She sat down on a grassy spot beside the cave's mouth and patted the place beside her.

As I sat down, she opened the basket. "Biscuits, butter, honey, coffee so hot it almost cracked the jar. I think it's still warm."

She watched me start eating, shaking her head when I offered her part of the food. "She wanted me to eat there, Wade."

She leaned back against the trunk of a small tree, looking

at the distances below. "Kirk Hyder came to the house early this morning. Routine, he said. He didn't expect me to be there and believed them when she and Hap told him I hadn't been around. Kirk thinks we slipped through, Wade."

"Fine."

"Giles was found very late last night. One of the cruising patrol cars saw the broken guard rail and investigated. They think it was a drunken-driving accident. Kirk mentioned this in his talk with Hap."

"Fine again," I said.

She plucked a blade of grass and began breaking it between her fingers. "We've got one final chance to get out of here, Wade."

"How?"

"Clarence."

I didn't say anything. I had finished the food. I put the empty coffee jar back in the basket.

"I sent my oldest brother into Big Hominy," she said. "I told him to call the hotel from a pay station and make sure no one overheard."

"What did you tell your brother to say?" I asked, hearing an unbidden coldness in my tone.

She turned her head to look at me. Her voice was low and quiet, "My brother will tell Clarence that I am at home and depending on him for help."

"And if Clarence asks about me?"

"My brother will say that I'm alone."

A silence came to the morning. She stood, crossed the short distance between us, and sat down with her legs folded under her.

"Vicky, he once told me the real test would begin when you

137

were free. That's what he wanted—your freedom for himself."

She reached up and traced the hairline around my temples with her fingertips. "You can have trust in me now," she said softly. "Do as you once asked me to do, Wade. Believe in me."

Oldham came to the McCall house shortly before noon. Mrs. McCall and Vicky sat in the barren front room. I stood in the kitchen, against the thin partition separating it from the front room. Trying to remain calm, I stood with the gun in my hands. A crack in the wall gave me a narrow view of the other room.

I saw Vicky move to the front door to meet him. He took her hands in his and looked at her a minute. "Thank heaven you're all right! I could have killed that crazy Calhoun when I heard about the break he pulled. Where is he, Vicky?"

"After the highway patrolman shot at us, he expressed his full intent to drive his car as long as there was a drop of gas in the tank."

"The punk! Ditching you like that."

Vicky stepped aside for him to enter the cabin. His brisk gaze missed no details. If he felt distaste for Hap's way of life, his face failed to show it.

"Clarence," Vicky said, "this is my mother. Mom, Mr. Oldham."

"Hello," Oldham said.

"Howdy," said Mrs. McCall. She stood up, hands clasped before her. "I reckon my daughter wants to speak to you in private, Mr. Oldham. Whatever they say, whatever has happened, she's a fine girl. She deserves any help you can give her."

"I'm sure of that, Mrs. McCall."

He watched Mrs. McCall shuffle from the cabin. Then he turned to Vicky, "We have quite a problem, my dear. Calhoun's presence would aggravate it. I'm speaking plainly. I considered the possibility of a trick, but I came anyway. I'm more than fond of you, and for that reason I had no choice. I couldn't have stayed away."

"You're a kind man, Clarence."

"Few people have ever said that about me," he said with a soft laugh. "But from you it's not enough."

"I'm very fond of you."

"That will suffice. I'm a realist. I've been called a cold-blooded realist. But I know how to be good to you, Vicky—provided I have assurance that you will repay me in kind."

Vicky gave a tight laugh. "You're a strange man! Who are you? Are you Lee Stamey?"

A moment of silence passed. He said, "Where did you hear that name?"

"In a roundabout way. Rock mentioned the name to Hap McCall. Hap told Wade. Wade told the sheriff. One of the deputies remarked to me that my deceased ex-husband had been carrying fifty thousand dollars stolen from a Jacksonville gambler named Lee Stamey. Then I began to remember things.

"Wade mentioned once that it was odd that you'd come here and cultivated my acquaintance shortly after Rock was reported back. Once I got to thinking about it, I remembered how you avoided the subject of your business and cut cold some hotel guests from Charlotte who tried to be friendly with you."

"Would it matter if I am Lee Stamey?" he asked.

"If you killed Rock, it would."

"You'd hate me for leaving you in the lurch. I wouldn't blame you, in the slightest. Had I killed him, the job would have been much less messy. You can believe that, Vicky. You can believe that I had no intention of killing him. Viewed realistically, from my position, the money was not worth a killing. The money can be recouped.

"I'll admit, Vicky, in the beginning you were a means to an end. I learned easily that you were Rock's ex-wife. I needed every channel of information I could cultivate. I needed to be as inconspicuous as possible. My plan was simple—locate Rock and retake the money at gunpoint.

"You must understand, Vicky, that in my business there are certain rules I must abide by. Failure to retake what Rock had stolen from me would have violated the first of those rules and caused me future trouble. Every punk with itching fingers would have regarded me as an easy mark."

"Yet you weren't intending to kill Rock."

"Only in the final extremity, in defending my own life. Knowing Rock, I was certain it wouldn't be necessary. Once he saw that I had caught him, he would surrender the money. His bravery was a cruel thing—when dealing with women or those weaker than himself.

"I thought you might be a help in locating him, Vicky. Then I began to see what you were really like. Very soon you were no longer a possible aid in finding Rock. You were a woman I had to have.

I could see that Vicky was shaken by Stamey's speech. I didn't want him talking to her any longer. He had been here a sufficient time for me to know he hadn't been followed.

I stepped to the doorway, the gun in my hand. Stamey

was standing with one hand on Vicky's shoulder, the other in the pocket of his sport jacket.

He heard the scrape of my left foot and turned toward me. "Well, hello, Calhoun," he said in a calm voice, his face devoid of expression. Then his jacket pocket exploded.

The bullet from his small gun punched me in the upper arm. I've heard that small guns don't carry shock force. This one had enough. I was spun halfway around. The gun fell to the plank flooring.

"A good gambler," Stamey said, "always hedges his bets. Kick the gun this way, Calhoun."

"Come and get it if you want it!"

He shrugged, crossed the room, and kicked the gun away from me. He walked to it and bent his knees to pick it up.

"Vicky," he said, "next time the stakes are very high, learn to control your facial expressions. You simply couldn't keep your eyes off that doorway."

She looked at me with misery in her face. "Wade . . ."

"Never mind him," Stamey said. "He's done his job perfectly. You're free—and I've won."

She stared at him.

"There's no need to look at me so strangely, my dear," he said. "This incident will be put behind us and forgotten. I'm hurt, yes, but grief doesn't alter my feelings for you. Now let's quit the talk and get going."

She didn't move. "I'm not going with you," she said in a low voice.

"I don't think you quite understand," he said. "I love you. I want you. I intend to have you. I'm the only person who can take you away from here. Who can shield you in the future from death, literally. Death in the gas chamber."

She sobbed, and the sound was filled with the despair of endless days and nights.

I moved toward Stamey without knowing I was doing it. I was able to see only his lean, corded neck. I could think only of how it would feel in the grip of my good hand.

He laughed softly. With a quick movement he was no longer before me. I tried to turn and meet him. He struck me with the gun he'd picked up, my own gun. He was very accurate. The blow above my temple was just accurate enough to erase all consciousness from my mind.

When my senses strained to focus themselves on the external world, I was first aware of a babble of sound. The sound gradually resolved into two distinct vocal expressions. A woman was moaning with grief and a man was crying with joy.

I opened my eyes. I was still in the McCall cabin, lying on a pallet of ragged quilts against the wall. The position of the sunlight coming through the window showed the time to be about mid-afternoon.

My shirt had been removed, by Mrs. McCall, I guessed, and iodine had been poured on the spot where Stamey's bullet had burned my arm. Naked to the waist, I realized that the canvas money belt was gone.

Without turning my head, I could see the table. Mrs. McCall sat at the far side, making her long, low sounds as she looked at Hap, who sat with his back to me.

He had the tabletop covered with thousand dollar bills. He smoothed them one by one; then he picked one up to wipe the tears from his cheeks and eyes.

"By hell," he cried in ecstasy, "I come home and find you

looking like a goggle-eyed perch at a moneybelt you've took from the belly of Wade Calhoun! Rock's money. The purty money I meant to have from the night me and Rock cracked a bottle and he made his brag. He wouldn't tell me. Even with a pistol whipping he wouldn't tell. Then I walk into my own house and there 'tis. By the devil, ain't it the beat!"

I went cold all over as I looked at Hap's jittering back. Everything was suddenly clear and simple. Hap had showed at the old Stillman cabin the night Kirk caught Vicky because Hap had been following the sheriff, watching developments and worrying. Wanting her, the hated child of another man, to pay for the crime Hap had committed himself.

Hap had denied seeing Rock within two days of Rock's death. But when Mrs. McCall had accompanied Evalina to my cell, Mrs. McCall had said Rock had bought whisky from Hap five days back—the afternoon before the murder!

The noise Vicky had heard outside the fish cabin had been Hap. And the mark down the side of Rick's jaw must have been made by a pistol sight as Hap, unable to control his greed for the money, had tried to pistol-whip the location of the money out of his drinking companion. One blow had been too hard, and Rock had died. Then Vicky had come to the cabin and Hap had seen a perfect out. He'd heard her drop the poker, noticed its location when he re-entered the cabin, and dipped it in Rock's blood.

A shadow touched the window-framed splash of sunlight falling across my chest. I looked up quickly. I saw Kirk Hyder outside.

I shifted my gaze toward the table. "How about me, Hap?"

He became rigid, with both hands hovering over the table.

He stood up, kicked his chair away, and said, "So you're awake, eh?"

"And listening. You killed Rock, framed Vicky, and you have the money. But I'm still here, Hap."

"Well, now, ain't you thinking right fanciful! How much trouble you figuring to cause me?"

"All I can, Hap."

He watched me struggle to my feet. He began laughing. "Won't be much! Ain't you heard? You're a fugitive. You've run out of the country. You're going to depart and disappear, you damn Calhoun. The mountains are big and lonely. The rocks are plentiful. You'll have a last resting place nobody will ever discover."

Kirk stepped into the front doorway.

Hap turned, saw the sheriff, and utter stupefaction showed on his face.

"My money," Hap whispered. "My money!" He flung himself across the table. He was sobbing anew; there was no joy in it now.

Mrs. McCall turned away. Kirk stood over Hap and reached out to lay his hand on Mrs. McCall's shoulder. "It's all right now, ma'am."

"He was going to kill Mr. Calhoun. Then I reckon he'd have threatened my children less'n I kept quiet. That was Hap's way."

"Yes," Kirk said, "that was Hap's way." He glanced at me. "Serve up the crow any way you like, Wade. I'm ready to eat plenty of it. The oldest McCall boy's in town making loose talk. He told some of the beer hounds he could tell them a tall story for a few rounds. They bought. He talked about Clarence Oldham coming here to get his sister. I

144

thought I'd better have a quiet look-see. I was after her, Wade. I didn't want to show my presence in case she was here."

He looked at Hap, who was prone and beaten on the table now.

"I've got the person I came after," Kirk said. "Not the person I thought I was coming after—but the right one."

"Now you've got to get her, Kirk. For me. She's with Stamey."

"Stamey?"

"Lee Stamey, alias Oldham. He forced her to go with him."

"I'll find her, Wade." He looked at me, his eyes telling me he was sorry for many things. "If I knew it would cost my life," he said, "I'd find her."

He spoke the words simply. He was not a man who made idle boasts.

And there came a day when workmen arrived at the old house that had once been the show place of Big Hominy. Shutters were opened. Blinds were removed and sunlight touched corners long dark. There was the smell of fresh paint and the ringing of hammers.

In the spring men with mowing blades cleared the weeds and brush that had encroached upon the once-green lawn. They prepared the ground and sowed the grass.

Vicky insisted on planting the flowers herself.